# Dies Irae:

# DAY OF WRATH

## William R. Forstchen

www.onesecondafter.com
www.dayofwrathbook.com
www.spectrumliteraryagency.com/forstchen.htm

*For those who stand watch against evil,*

*for the two who told me I must write this book,*

*and for a Third who inspired me to not turn back.*

# FOREWORD

This is a book that I did not want to write.

Several years back, I wrote a novel about the threat to our national infrastructure from an EMP (electromagnetic pulse) attack. *One Second After* was published by Tor/Forge, and became a New York Times bestseller. I never anticipated its impact and what some now claim: its leading role in the creation of the so-called "prepper movement." After that, and far more pleasurable in the writing, was my next work, *Pillar to the Sky*, a novel about a positive future which we can fashion with a renewed support of our space program. Both books were challenging in different ways, but never hit to such a visceral level as this book now does.

Only weeks before this ebook, *Day of Wrath*, hits publication, the murderous forces of ISIS swept into northern Iraq and unleashed a reign of terror that this historian sees as a campaign that makes Hitler's and Stalin's fanatical followers look like amateurs. I am an historian of warfare; I often describe my job as similar to that of an oncologist. I study that which kills and hope that one day humanity will find a cure. When one matures from being a young man to middle aged, and suddenly the scourge of war is no longer something that you will bear personally on the battlefield, but instead will be borne by your children, by young students in your classroom whom you come to love, the fear of it strikes far deeper and is far more poignant.

A few months back during a Saturday afternoon discussion with two who are very dear to my heart, the twin topics of ISIS with its barbaric outrages and the security crisis on our southern border came up. By the end of that conversation, both challenged me to write what became this book.

They argued and I had to agree that when a blood-lusting regime is openly declaring that they will take their murderous rampage into the heartland of America, combined with the fact that our border security is in tatters, it is time to take notice. (And any political leader who says that our borders are "secure" is either a liar or senile.)

Osama bin Laden made clear his intentions for us long before 9/11. Hitler made clear his intentions to all whom he declared were "racial inferiors." The list of warnings from such hideous murderers goes back to the first pages of recorded history. Those who did not listen to such warnings eventually learned of their folly. Are we doing the same today?

ISIS, or whatever it now calls itself as this book is released, has made clear its intent: our deaths and that of our friends and allies in Europe and Israel. Beyond that, the deaths of all who do not adhere to their interpretation of the Koran, including fellow Sunni Muslims who they view as "weak in their faith," and Shi'ites.

What is clear regarding ISIS and others like them: Their intent is to convert the world, both "Muslim" and "Infidel," and if we are not willing to convert, then we must die. Second, and it surprises me that Western feminists are not more attuned and reactive to this issue, women are subservient on earth and are nothing more than objects of sexual fulfillment for martyred jihadists in their paradise. To say otherwise is to mislead, which their interpretation of the Koran states is acceptable. To mislead and lie to the infidel is acceptable until dominance over the "infidel" is achieved, at which point all must submit, convert, or die.

The twentieth century was the great battlefield of

western liberalism, in its classical sense, against the forces of totalitarianism. In his seminal work, *1984*, George Orwell's fictional character "O'Brien", a leader of the "thought police," declared that our fate would forever be the boot of a totalitarian state smashing in the face of humanity. We came damn close to that fate and that threat still exists. I believe the great struggle of the twenty-first century is now unfolding on the dust-covered plains of Iraq, where ISIS runs rampant, and could very well be fought in Europe and on our own soil. It is the struggle between a medieval murderous cult, filled with hatred against what Abraham Lincoln declared to be "the last best hope of mankind."

There is a subtext within these pages that transcends ISIS; I'll leave that for you to find. Recall the words of a politician who declared that any crisis presents political opportunity as well. You can accept my concern about ISIS alone, or with this other concern; at least in what is still a free Republic: that is something for you to decide.


One can find evidence of just how evil ISIS truly is in very little time. Turn off your television and its reality shows. Go and face a true reality. Run a few internet searches of what ISIS, and those like it, truly is. The information can easily be found for, unlike the Nazis and the NKVD of Stalin, this cult does not hide its crimes. They gleefully post videos on a regular basis of their torturing, beheading, crucifying and executing thousands. Look evil in the eye and have the stomach and courage to stare back and say "no more." To become aware, no matter how disturbing that reality is, is the first step to the resistance that we must be prepared to make in response.

The final decision is in doubt. We can continue to

sleep, to not face reality, and to turn a blind eye or extend tolerance to cults of hate, or we can openly call evil for what it is and stand against it. There was a time when we did not hesitate to say that some things are indeed evil. Why do we fear to do so now?

In closing: The opinion I voice here is my own, not that of friends, of colleagues, or of the college where I am privileged to teach. I hated writing this book. I had looked forward to a relaxing summer after working on a morally uplifting book about the promise of our space program. I did not want to write this one, but, as I expressed to friends, I feared that if I did not write it, and this nightmare happened, which it surely can, I would be responsible in some way for remaining silent. If you read on from here, it will not be an enjoyable experience. I hope that it will make enough of us think things through to ensure not only the safety of our children, but of our Republic as well. And, as always with such works that speculate a dark future, I hope that awareness will bring preparedness and thus the nightmare never happens. If so, the effort will have been worth it.

William R. Forstchen
August 10, 2014

*"Dies iræ, dies illa, dies tribulationis et angustiæ, dies calamitatis et miseriæ, dies tenebrarum et caliginis, dies nebulæ et turbinis, dies tubæ et clangoris super civitates munitas et super angulos excelsos."*
*That day is a day of wrath, a day of tribulation and distress, a day of calamity and misery, a day of darkness and obscurity, a day of clouds and whirlwinds, a day of the trumpet and alarm against the fenced cities, and against the high bulwarks...*
Zephaniah 1: 15-16

*"And fight with them until there is no more fitna (disorder, unbelief) and religion should be only for Allah."*
Koran sura 8:39

*"I will cast terror into the hearts of those who disbelieve. Therefore strike off their heads and strike off every fingertip of them."*
Koran sura 8:12

# Dies Irae:
# DAY OF WRATH

William R. Forstchen

# Table of Contents

# CHAPTER ONE

*7:25 a.m., Near Portland, Maine*

"We have lived with the abnormal for so long, we believe it to be normal."

Bob Petersen gazed at the screen for a moment, not sure if he should continue. He had long ago come to the conclusion that blogging and posting commentary on Facebook was a supreme act of self-indulgence. A few friends might read it, act polite, and give a thumbs up. There had been a time, before he made the wiser career choice of going into IT education versus creative writing, that he fancied he might make it as an author. After all, he lived in Maine, home to a lot of writers, and had even attended a few writers' workshops. The workshops were finally enough to convince him to pursue a more stable line of work, especially after he met Kathy, married, and started to think about a family.

Facebook for him was not a place to vent... but today, this morning...? The news of the day, echoing from the kitchen where Kathy was preparing lunches for their daughter Wendy and him to take to school, was yet another overwhelming litany of bad news and it triggered a sense of foreboding.

The offensive by ISIS in Iraq was on the march again. More images of mass executions, beheadings, and Christians being crucified. These were the horrors committed under the guidance of the one who had declared himself to be the returner of the caliphate, a man who, to Bob, was every bit as threatening as a Hitler or bin Laden.

Bob's younger brother had died over there back in 2004. For what, in light of this latest news?

Reports echoed from the television in the kitchen about

1

the border along Texas: not all trying to cross were refugees from impoverished Central America. New indications were that it was a route Middle Eastern terrorists were using to infiltrate... but for what? A commentator on his preferred news network just last night stated that he felt the "perfect storm" was about to explode.

It had been a somewhat sleepless night. Kathy always told him he worried too much about what he could not fix, but this morning he was up an hour earlier than usual to just jot down some thoughts. It was as if some inner voice whispered that he had to make a statement now; to do it this morning before he left for work. Later in the day he would look back at it, and hopefully today would be an ordinary day like all the others across the years, and he'd be slightly embarrassed that he had posted these ramblings.

"We expect to be lied to," he continued to write. "In fact, the truth is so rare these days that we think it is spoken only as a maneuver of the moment to cover yet another lie. Our leaders tell us to believe in them, that they do all for our good. They tell us that they fight for our rights while they travel about in entourages costing millions for their monthly vacations. They tell us to conserve, for all is running short, while their private jets take them to their next gathering. What are proclaimed to be our entertainers are experts on all things simply because they act a role in a movie. Their role model to our youth is one of dissipation, mocking any of us who try to teach our children any type of values.

"News last night was of yet another thirty-thousand dollar-a-plate fundraiser to pay for yet more lies to blanket their hypocrisy, to opiate us while the worshipful media stands awestruck. Every night is Oscar night in

2

Washington with some self-congratulatory award. Every day, a new scandal of the day (at least for that twenty four hour news cycle) is examined with about as much critical skill as that of entertainment reporters gasping about who left her husband for a new affair. Politics are merged with entertainment and entertainment with politics, though one used to be only for diversion while the other truly was, and still is, a matter of life and death.

"The death of a second-rate actor to drugs draws more media and mourning than the sealed metal boxes returning from the Middle East."

He paused after writing that line. The morning that he and Kathy were preparing to head to Dover Air Force base, to greet the returning casket of his brother, the headline news was about the accidental death of yet another entertainer to a drug overdose. Several days later, the media lavished attention on tearful fans weeping at the funeral. His brother and four others of his squad were buried that day, and it hardly made local news. The only ones who wept at his brother's funeral were his family, friends from high school, and a comrade who had been assigned to escort the body, or what was left of the body… they never opened the casket… home from Iraq.

He sat in silent reflection for a moment, then continued to write.

"The new daily scandal of Washington has become business as usual, to be forgotten a day later with a new scandal, a new affair. The reality show has become reality, and the real world an increasingly anesthetized dream to be ignored.

"And those of us who dare to question do so with voices lowered, for in America today the worst sin of all, the real sin, is no longer racism or hatred… it is simply fear that you might offend.

"The Republic was not founded by those who feared to offend. It was not created by those who were afraid to fight back. Is it time to fight back? But how do we fight back? What do we fight back against? How do we fight back?"

"Hey Bob, you're gonna be late!"

He looked at the screen, scrolled back over what he just wrote, highlighting it, and poised his finger over the delete button. Why bother? I'm just pissed off this morning. Vent here and I get eighty comments back, most of them inane, asking what the hell is bugging me. It will disappear while everyone prefers to see the latest video clip of who twerked her ass last night at some awards ceremony or had a dress "malfunction," and after all, we are being told that all the scandals are phony anyhow.

"Come on!"

He stood up, looked again at the screen, and let his finger drift from delete to enter. He hit the enter button, posting his musings, and felt a twinge of regret and embarrassment. Which friends would be offended today?

Kathy was waiting out in the kitchen, making the loving gesture of holding out a cup of coffee. She was wearing what he called her frumpy bathrobe, her hair still something a tangle and no makeup... all factors which made her even more lovable to him. Given their "surprise" a year ago, she had resumed the role of staying at home for a few more years.

He gladly took the cup and drained it halfway in two gulps. She had mixed it nearly half and half coffee and cream, even though she was on his case about the cholesterol in the cream.

She had taken on the ritual of getting up an hour earlier than he to cook breakfast for their older daughter and make his coffee. He simply couldn't stand food other than some caffeine to provide the jolt for waking up to face the outside world, after, of course, he engaged for a few minutes in his fantasy of being a writer.

They had met in their junior year at the University of Maine in Bangor, had scandalized their very Catholic parents by living together their senior year, and then stilled that scandalizing by marrying a week after graduation. Kathy had been a secondary math education major, he a computer education major. He had taken his father's advice to "get a degree that will get you a job," and chase the dream of writing afterwards.

They had actually scored positions at the same school, in a suburb of Portland, teaching side by side for four years until Wendy came along. Kathy had taken a couple of years off for their first daughter, then gone back to teaching… until their mid-life surprise of two years back. Every morning now he could see her duality. She adored being a full-time mother again, but as she handed him his cup of coffee to pack him off for another day at school, he could sense her longing, her missing of "their kids" at Joshua Chamberlain Middle School.

The day was one of those glorious Maine autumn days, a touch of frost was on the car out in the driveway, and he remembered fondly their first year of teaching: leaving the apartment, he would go out first, when it was down near zero degrees, to scrape the car and heat it up before she dashed to its warmth.

Their daughter Wendy stood behind her mother. She bore such a striking resemblance to the family album photos of her mother at the same age: lanky, long-legged and coltish. Her red hair was tied back in a pony tail; already the clear signs were there of the stunning beauty she would grow into, but she was still very much "daddy's girl," even though she tried not to let that show, especially around her friends. And she was obviously ticked off that Dad was running late. Her morning gossip circle awaited in homeroom. She could barely spare a quick glance to her dad as he pecked her on the cheek, then she was back to her cell phone, texting away and chortling about how someone named Janey was definitely going to get it good today for being caught kissing the boyfriend of some girl named Hallie.

He glanced at Kathy and said nothing. Wasn't that supposed to start when they were fifteen or so? Even though he taught middle school, he still looked at his charges as children, though popular culture had been putting girls such as Miley Cyrus at age fifteen on the cover of Vanity Fair for years.

Kathy made no comment about the scandal at school as she tucked a packed lunch into Wendy's backpack, leaned up, and kissed Bob on the cheek.

"Have a good day."

He kissed her back and looked over her shoulder to Shelly, their one-year-old, sitting in a high chair at the kitchen table. She was happily smearing her face and hair with chocolate pudding, laughing away at whatever was the inner delight of one-year-olds when putting on disgusting displays.

Wendy spared a quick glance at her kid sister and gave a grunt of disgust.

"You were just as gross at that age," Bob offered. She simply rolled her eyes.

"I was perfect compared to that," Wendy bragged, but he could see a bit of an affectionate smile regarding "the brat's" display.

"Wanna trade jobs for the day?" Kathy sighed, eyeing Shelly then back at the two of them heading off to school.

"You were the one who said it'd be fun to have

another," he replied a bit defensively.

"Yeah," was all he could muster out of her. "Just one day, come on! You guys can stay here, clean up the smeared chocolate, change the diapers, watch that damn purple dinosaur dancing around on television, and I can at least have a five-minute intellectual conversation with some twelve-year-olds."

She looked at the two wistfully, eyebrows raised, head tilted to one side, and with a trace of an impish smile, the look that could always nail Bob and leave him a bit weak in the knees even after all these years. He realized she was actually half serious and that if he said yes, she'd dash off to the bedroom, slap some makeup on and be out the door with Wendy, telling their principal that she was his sub for the day.

Wendy looked at her mother with sympathy but her glance indicated that she also thought her mother's appeal must be insane.

"Intellectual conversation? Seventh grade? Come on Mom, you gotta be kidding."

"Next year," was all Bob could offer, not sure if she was really lamenting or just trying to make them feel guilty as they headed out for another day in the world.

Kathy smiled, that same winsome smile that had caught him on the day they met when he could have sworn that her eyes actually sparkled with light the first time he gazed into them. She brushed back an errant wisp of red hair from her face, leaving a smear of chocolate pudding on her jawline and neck, which made him laugh softly and half kiss, half lick it off her.

"Don't do that," she whispered so that Wendy, standing expectantly by the door would not hear, "You'll get me thinking and I'm stuck here alone without you."

"Maybe tonight," he whispered.

"Come on Dad, we're late!"

The two peeked over at their twelve-year-old standing at the doorway who gazed at them with a look of exasperation and judgmental embarrassment at parents who act too affectionately.

Kathy pushed him away.

"Get going…"

He paused, drawn to the television screen on the kitchen counter.

"Today's lead stories we're covering after the break. The shooting incident yesterday at Robert Morrison High School outside Syracuse, New York, that left four people dead and ten wounded is drawing increasing scrutiny with the report released at seven this morning by an anonymous official that the gunman had a letter on his body in Arabic that proclaimed that the time of the jihad promised by ISIS had come. Federal officials on the scene are dismissing the report and urging calm. All schools in the Syracuse area are closed for the day…"

Across the bottom of the screen, the ticker tape was providing a brief account of the deaths of three border security guards the night before near Austin, Texas, in what one witness claimed was a professional attack and not just a random shooting incident.

He took it in, saw the look of worry in Kathy's eyes. Anyone who taught in a public school, especially couples who taught in the same school, talked about "what if it happens in our school?" He gingerly leaned over to kiss Shelly on the top of the head, making sure she didn't smear him with pudding. He wrinkled his nose. The kid stank, and he suppressed a gag. It was definitely one aspect of fatherhood he was an utter failure at and he was glad that he was heading out the door rather than being called up for diaper service.

"You little monster, love you," he sighed and gazed back at Kathy and smiled lovingly. Wendy was already at the car.

"I'm late," was all he could say as an excuse, and was out the door into the chilly Maine October morning. He looked back again and blew a kiss to Kathy, a tradition they had followed ever since the first night they had spent together.

It was the last time they would see each other alive.

*Near Raqqa, Syria*
*#diesirae631: Sword One: Four hours, Sword Two: Four and a Half Hours, Allahu Akbar.*

# CHAPTER TWO

*7:45 a.m., Near Portland, Maine*

Bob parked the car that he and Kathy called "the indulgence" in his usual spot at Joshua Chamberlain Middle School. The red 350Z seemed a bit extreme for someone getting by on the pay of a high school teacher, but they had purchased it used years ago before Wendy was born, in fact just a couple of weeks before finding out Kathy was pregnant. The car had remained, even though it was totally impractical for a new family. The more utilitarian Subaru SUV took the parking place alongside it in the driveway of the small three bedroom home they had purchased eight years ago.

It was not the existence they had talked about when they first met and had fallen in love. The plan had been, after they married and landed their jobs at the middle school in a suburb of Portland, that after several years he'd go back to grad school, then leave teaching for a far better paying job in the corporate world. She would then pursue an advanced degree in math and teach at the college level. With that accomplished, perhaps his writing would even take off some day. Making it as a writer was, as they called it, a "Cinderella Fantasy," but it had sounded nice at the time.

Then Wendy came along, and as is so typical of life, the game played out with the two teaching and saying to each other that in twenty-five years, when they could collect retirement and Wendy was off to college, they would resume those dreams. And then the mid-life surprise of Shelly put that plan on further hold.

As he made the motions of opening the car door to get out, he caught a few seconds of eye contact with Wendy, and he had no complaints. He and Kathy had a loving marriage, a rarity, it seemed, in this world, and two girls who were blessed with good health. Sure it was a grind, going in early and staying late at school, and finances were tight with Kathy staying home. But at this moment, on this peaceful autumn day in Maine, his daughter flashed him a shy smile and he felt blessed and grateful for it.

"I'm late, Daddy," Wendy complained as she opened the door and started to get out. Gone were the days of walking her into primary school, holding hands, and sharing a hug. Perhaps she sensed his disappointment because she glanced back at him and gave him a toothy grin, a reminder that the big expense to come this year would be braces.

"Love you, Dad," she offered and then was off, running to the side of one of her friends. Wendy began showing a text message on her phone, which she'd have to shut down once inside the building and both of them giggled. He sighed.

Once she was out of sight he opened the compartment between the seats. Something about the news today... No, not just today, the news every day of late, had forced a decision that only Kathy knew about. He pulled out a Ruger .380 from the glove compartment and slipped it into his pants pocket.

Even though he had a permit to carry a concealed weapon, he was now in felony violation of both Federal law and the laws of the State of Maine. If discovered, he would lose his teaching license and face up to five years in prison.

If found out? If found out by someone simply seeing the pistol, if it slipped out of his pocket as he squatted down to pick something up, if the pants he was wearing were a bit too tight and some sharp-eyed coworker got suspicious and ran to tell the principal... The principal would summon him while calling the police, who would then come and pat him down, handcuff him and take him to jail. If found out, he would be in prison, license to teach revoked for a lifetime, and pay fines. The national media would show a viral video of him being led out in handcuffs. The only crime more reprehensible in a school: to sexually stalk or use a student, which he felt did indeed deserve capital punishment rather than prison with rehabilitation therapy and a sentence that was likely shorter than the one he would face.

Caught by a student wandering into his classroom after-hours to find him having an affair with another teacher? Embarrassed dismissal. Embezzling? Perhaps a fine and quiet termination.

Incompetence in the classroom, which he also felt was a crime worthy of punishment? As long as the incompetent teacher's students jumped through the hoops of testing, no big deal. When he did complain once about another faculty member who, as he said, "could not figure out his I.Q. unless he looked at the bottom of his shoe," the response was, "Mr. Iverson retires in six more years, so just let it go for now. Besides, the union would kick up a fuss." Being a teacher, Bob was at least able to force the issue with his own daughter by insisting on a transfer to another teacher, but for the other hundred kids stuck in Iverson's class day after day? Well, at least in six more years he would be gone.

The gun? Why the gun?

He did not buy the years of administrative instructions, coming from "experts" in the main office, while day after day he looked into the eyes of his students and inwardly asked, "What do I do?" if the nightmare came to Chamberlain Middle School. He did not buy the counterintuitive logic that if there were a gunman in the building, to lock the door, lie on the floor, and pray. Well, not actually pray, for after all this was a public school, but he could at least insist upon a moment of silence as they waited to get shot.

In whispered conversations with only a few other teachers and Kathy, the conclusion returned again and again to the same point. Up until 9/11 all were drilled that if on a hijacked plane, sit back, relax, take a Xanax, listen to those in charge, and all would be well. (Unless you were Jewish and the hijacker a Muslim. If so, ditch your passport and say your name is Smith.)

And then there was United flight #93: the fourth hijacking on that black day of days. The cell phone calls informing the passengers on that doomed flight that it was time to fight back. They fought and died, and in so doing likely saved thousands on the ground.

After that day, he believed that it wasn't just the billions spent on security that had resulted in not a single hijacking in American airspace since 9/11. It was the fundamental realization that if anyone tried to take a plane, two hundred ordinary Americans on that plane *would fight back*. That, more than any other factor, deterred the enemy who now sought other targets, in the same manner that so many had once learned that rather than whine about a bully in an elementary school yard, the final and most convincing answer was to fight back on the spot. A comparison of the hijackings in the thirteen years prior to 9/11 versus after 9/11, to Bob, was proof enough of how to respond.

So he broke federal and state law this morning: the law that experts had said for years was the only answer. To be defenseless? To lock a door, to wait and pray? He could no longer believe that argument. In whispered conversations with others he argued that he was a teacher, and, above all other considerations, his first duty was to protect his students no matter what. If need be, he would face prison for doing that duty. Better that than to be passive as a sheep and watch as the lambs in his charge get slaughtered.

He had not taken his decision lightly or in a cavalier manner as some macho idiots would do. He had legally purchased the weapon and taken the required course to carry a concealed weapon (though of course it was illegal to do so on school property). Kathy had as well, for she was a teacher at the time they had made the decision. They then took the advanced courses offered by a local firearms store regarding safety and how and when to use the weapon he was about to carry into the school in violation of the law. In his mind, it was a moral choice. If ever the children in his charge were threatened, he believed that the first responsibility of a teacher, transcending all other responsibilities, was to protect.

He popped the magazine, double checking that no round was actually chambered in the weapon, slipped it back in, and pocketed the gun. It carried six hollow point rounds and resided in a holster pocket that Kathy had sewn inside the right pocket of his jeans. That done, he exited the car, opened the back hatch for his book bag, and, in what was now an unconscious gesture, ran his hand down his right side to make sure the weapon was properly holstered and not visible.

He walked into the school, ignoring the warning signs posted on all school doors that Joshua Chamberlain Middle School was a gun-free zone, and smiled a genuinely warm and friendly greeting to Charlie, the sixty-year-old security and resource officer who smiled a greeting in return. The two paused as Charlie asked about

"Miss Kathy" and they joked about the diaper he had avoided changing. He then traveled the short distance to his classroom and office in the IT wing, kids rushing past him laughing and locker doors slamming. It was the start of another typical day at Joshua Chamberlain Middle School just outside of Portland, Maine.

## 8:45 a.m., Portland, Maine

They had driven up from Atlantic City, New Jersey, the day before and stayed at a fairly upscale hotel just off the Falmouth exit of Interstate 95, arriving just after eight in the evening the day before. They had been admonished repeatedly in their training to make sure they had a good eight hours' sleep when the final hours came. But none had done so. Regardless of their faith, how could one sleep soundly when knowing it was the last night they would spend on this earth, and, come the following day, they would die as holy martyrs?

Regardless of all they had seen in their years of holy war, regardless of just how many they had killed, from putting the round of a Kalashnikov into the forehead of a grandmother who had closed her eyes in the final seconds whispering a Christian prayer as she waited for death, to a screaming woman who knew her fate after being raped, to an infant whose throat was so easy to cut when asleep in the cradle, this they knew for certain: their own time had come. The last hours of life were drawing to an end, their fears stilled by the promises of their caliph of what awaited them in paradise.

How painful would death be? They had seen men and women burned alive and the first time they had witnessed that, even though it was an infidel, there was a moment of flinching and wondering how one's own flesh would smell if fate determined that they would die trapped in flames?

16

How intense would be the pain? The caliph promised them that if trapped in fire as a holy martyr, the flames would feel as cooling as a mountain stream as they winged to paradise.

Some had even driven the nails to crucify Christians, a most fitting death for those of that absurd faith. The infidels were too weak to do the same to them but the thoughts did linger about the moment of their death. Would it hurt? Rather than pain would it become bliss unlike any they had known upon earth, and be a foreshadowing of the eternal bliss given to one who died in jihad? All pleasures denied to them on earth would at last be theirs: pure women, ever virgin for their desire to never be taken before them and thus soiled by another man. If the woman given to them was not pleasing and submissive in all ways, they could be cast into oblivion at any time, for such women in paradise existed solely for the pleasure of holy jihadists. Awaiting them would also be boys with soft pliant bodies and the faces of angels to be used as desired. There awaited every fruit to feast upon and fountains of strong drink as promised by the prophet and his living envoy, the caliph. Such thoughts now strengthened their hearts for the task ahead and stilled their fears, filling them with the joy of anticipation.

The journey had begun six months ago starting with a container ship out of a Middle Eastern port. No one involved in this plan had traveled by air. Thus they avoided the random chance of a database check, face recognition software, or a capture. Instead, over a hundred jihadists had departed their homeland on random dates, never in a group, using a roundabout journey to finally arrive at Vera Cruz, Mexico.

With all of the attention focused on airlines, the obvious alternative was container ships where chances were less than five percent that the ship would even be checked. During the spring offensive of ISIS into Iraq, over half a billion in hard currency had been captured: not just useless paper but actual gold. Bin Laden had boasted that his day of glory had been purchased for little more than half a million in American currency. What could half a billion buy? Most certainly the cooperation of the drug cartels of Central America to help pass along, at a cost of two million each, the jihadists from the port of Vera Cruz to the "mules" and "coyotes" who would take them across the porous border of America. Half the fee on signing, half on delivery to their handlers in America. And, unlike some financial deals engaged in by the cartels, even they were fearful of the wrath of ISIS if there were a betrayal or a failure.

Only two conspirators had been waylaid while traveling through Mexico to the border. To show their good faith to the Middle Easterners, the cartel had cut the throats of those responsible, along with the "federal police" who had refused to accept the bribes to look the other way.

All electronic chatter was to be silenced except for the final moments. All of the jihadists had their plans, their marching orders, their pickup points, their transfers, and their final missions. They knew whom they would link up with and where all was laid out and memorized before leaving the training center in eastern Syria. Nothing was in writing. Nothing was transmitted. All had absolute faith in their leader, that they would bring their vengeance to America. Those who had doubted, those who had voiced concerns, or who had tried to back away once initiated into the secret, were already dead and buried in unmarked graves in the desert.

For nearly thirteen years there had been hundreds of

boasts by other groups, other so-called jihadists, but no successful attack had been launched within the United States since 9/11. The few attacks planned and initiated had been intercepted because of their own foolish mistakes.

But the boasting had served a purpose. It had lulled the enemy. It had lulled those who kept watch but were not allowed to tell the American media of their successes. Even more so, it had lulled the sheep of their society. The absence of a successful attack in more than a decade had lulled them to believe they actually were safe.

Even if the enemy did see something suspicious, it had been drilled into them for years not to be rude, to be politically correct, not to point and shout a warning, out of fear that they would be called phobic or racist.

At the same time, the jihadists had learned from the mistakes of the once-respected bin Laden and those who followed him. They learned from the victories of their enemies, because those victories often resulted in a repeating of the same actions over and over. Yes, they did have strengths with all of their technology: their drones and their cell phone call intercepts. Therefore, infiltrate the target as low-tech as possible. Approach with utmost stealth, like a shadow in the desert at night, and not brazenly, walking under the noonday sun.

In the preceding months, the way paved by money looted from the successful offensive into Iraq, there were careful transfers of each jihadist across the border.

All fighters had been carefully screened and selected for the mission. Thousands of foreign fighters had joined the ranks of ISIS, some of whom were frustrated with the increasingly conservative ways of Al-Qaeda. The leader's main criteria for selecting his jihadists for this mission: their willingness to die in jihad, a rigorous vetting back to their birth, and numerous references to ensure that not one of them was an agent or traitor infiltrating from the West.

They had to demonstrate a near-perfect ability to blend into the western world. It amazed him how the attackers of 9/11 were, upon reflection, far too obvious. That risk would not be run this time. Their command of English had to be near flawless. They had to be able to put on a business suit, walk through a crowd, and no one would take a second look. If need be, they could even mimic adherence to an infidel faith and speak warmly of their love for Jews. This was no violation of faith, of course. The renowned scholar Al-Bukhari explained such logic when he commented on sura 3.28 of the Koran that, "We smile in the face of some people although our hearts curse them." And, of course, there was sura 3.54, which declared that the best deceiver of all was Allah himself. Such words were armor for the hearts and souls of his jihadists to infiltrate the evil heart of the West.

Those who actually at some point in their lives had lived in the belly of the beast, the world of the infidels, attending western schools, he personally checked as to their faith and willingness to die as holy warriors. They had to show him their ability to fight and kill without second thought or mercy. During some of the thousands of executions in Iraq, he had made sure that those being considered for this attack took part in them: they were required to wield the knife for beheadings and drive the nails for crucifixions. No double agent would do this. If they blanched, they were no longer considered. Those who failed the tests were dead before the sun set.

They were required to shave their beards, their clothing tailored by experts, learn to speak in the latest dialect of decadent America, and drill relentlessly on their created identities. In public, they would gossip about the latest game or whorish starlet, even drink a beer with dinner in a barbecue restaurant. If offered forbidden food, they were to eat it without hesitation. He reinforced the rulings in the Koran that those on jihad were exempt from all sins. Only in the privacy of their heart would there be prayers, until the final hour before the assault began. Until then, blend in with your foe so adroitly that he will not question. If there is a question, he will fear to ask it because that is their culture.

None of the targets was within fifty kilometers of a major city. That was another strength of their plan: to avoid the major cities where the random chance of passing someone on a street might trigger a recognition by someone trained well enough to recognize the wolf moving silently amongst the sheep. The caliph reinforced that the slightest failure or lapse in the United States would result in damnation and execution and, if shown to be egregious, their families would pay the price as well.

Of course there was always the random chance of something going wrong: a traffic accident, a drunk driver, perhaps an American veteran of Afghanistan or Iraq who just might take a second look. And such an event did happen. An angry American veteran claimed he recognized a jihadist. The jihadist left the fast food restaurant with his American handler, the vet following and shouting a challenge. The handler reacted brilliantly and as trained, shouting back that the American was a racist, even as he thanked him for his service to our country. His cries of racism prompted those who were standing nearby and watching to back off and to even offer apologies, warning the veteran to leave the two innocent men alone.

Gradually the thirty-plus teams came together around the country, going to ground several hundred miles or more away from what would be their final targets. The teams were made up of three to seven jihadists, depending on their target and mission. The cover of some was to attend a trade show or convention. Others were on vacation, such as the team assigned to the state of Maine, which stayed for a week in Atlantic City where they gambled and play-acted that they were rich Dubai bastards out for a little fun, while waiting for the count-down, waiting for the coded message that would not even be sent via the internet.

The message that the attack was to be unleashed was actually a news story about one of their leaders being executed as a traitor. After weeks of staying well-hidden in the midst of the enemy, the news story came. It was first broadcasted by Al-Jazeera that one of the top commanders of ISIS had been denounced as a CIA spy and beheaded. It was picked up by the American media within the hour, Fox News had experts on within three hours, speculating that a breakdown was occurring within ISIS, and perhaps the enemy was turning on itself. ISIS even released footage of the execution to lend credence to the story. The man executed had been marked by their leader for termination anyhow; his faith was wavering. The execution was the signal to initiate the attack two mornings later, just before noon, eastern time. No transmission, no internet, a news story as the only signal.

The team assigned to Maine left Atlantic City that same day, skirting wide around New York City and staying within the speed limit, looking like five businessmen traveling to a conference, and always speaking English. They purchased cell phones at convenience stores but turned them off. They stowed golf bags in the back of the SUV for their vacation jaunt to Maine while other teams headed to a beach house party in

Daytona, a family reunion in Marietta, Georgia, a conference in Springfield, Illinois, a trip to see friends in Oklahoma City, and a trip to buy a boat outside of Seattle.

The tools they needed had been carefully moved weeks earlier, one piece or several at a time. For the Maine team, an American handler who had been positioned far ahead of the jihadists who would carry out the attacks went to a famous mail order house in Freeport for fishing supplies and then purchased additional equipment. American handlers, so called "sleeper agents," had infiltrated into America long before the plans for the attack were laid out and trained for. They were men with clean records who purchased guns across several months at gun shows or on the used market. Never in bulk, just one or two at a time, and paid for with cash. Ironically, a number of weapons originated from the infamous Fast and Furious scheme, gleefully given to them by the cartels helping to transport jihadists across Mexico to the American border.

The Kevlar bulletproof vests and other equipment were purchased one at a time from a number of different sources so as to not draw notice. Some were found on Craigslist. They moved the weapons to the more than thirty jump-off points for attack by tucking them under suitcases, inside golf bags, and among the overloaded vehicle of a family with several children in tow going on a vacation trip. The jihadists who would actually do the killing, until the day before the attack, were free of the encumbrance of a weapon in case of the random chance of being stopped. The handlers would be their drivers on the day of the attack and if random chance resulted in their being caught prior to the attack, they would appear to be either gang members moving weapons for M-13 or some other cartel gang, or just lone lunatics.

But none were caught. Security had held so far. Each

team worked in isolation; only a few in ISIS knew the entire plan. If any one team was stopped prior to the day, the confession was the intent to shoot a plane down as it took off, thus focusing the typical American media panic on airports.

They were forbidden under threat of eternal damnation to breathe a word of what they knew of the plan. But two broke that rule: one with a team north of New Orleans, the other, in Las Vegas, who got drunk and slipped up in public during an argument with an equally drunk marine who was on leave and made a comment about "damned ragheads."

Las Vegas, which, as the heart of America's decadence, was one of the most ideal of targets and was coveted by all while in training. However, it was decided the attack in that region would hit in the area of Reno, sticking to the plan not to strike within any major city. As the brawl erupted, the fool had spoken in Arabic that soon the infidel would truly learn to fear, for the day of wrath was at hand. His comrades uttered apologies as they dragged him back to his room. The next day at a cheap hotel on the far side of town, he died from an injection to simulate a drug overdose. The same was done to the too-loquacious one in New Orleans. Speedball overdoses were, of course, part of the American scene. Overdosed bodies, even Middle Eastern ones, rarely drew notice beyond a local news report. So far there had been no wider reaction. Such things surfaced in the news for a single cycle then as quickly disappeared.

In the final forty-eight hours, the teams moved to their strike positions. After months of planning, tensions began to run high, as they always do before battle. One team member had actually gone off half-cocked in Syracuse. For reasons the rest of his unit did not know, he had driven away from the hotel where they had rendezvoused that morning with the handler who had transported their weapons and equipment. He had slipped out, taking the handler's car, and hit their target on his own. This had sent out a ripple of warning. Before he was killed, he had murdered four and wounded ten.

They had been trained for the possibility that one of their team might be spotted and captured, but not for one of them going off on his own crazed spree just hours before the real attack was to take place. The group immediately split up, going underground to sweat out the final twenty-four hours and not breaking silence. Each would now have to act on his own as best he could, but their main target was abandoned.

As to the activity of the team south of Austin, which the American media was reporting as the murder of three border security guards, it had been a random pullover by border patrol that had resulted in the three agents being shot within seconds and the team fleeing. Disciplined, they had slunk into the desert to sit out the final hours before resuming the mission.

So two out of the thirty-plus teams were in some state of disarray, but those in a hotel off the Falmouth exit near Portland, Maine, were ready. The cell phones had been activated. The twitter account, long dormant, was activated and the one lone tweet came in, time-stamped 7:45: *#diesirae631: Four hours, Sword One. Four Hours and a Half Hours, Sword Two. Allahu Akbar.*

There were three hours to go. The Falmouth, Maine, team contained units of both Sword One and Sword Two. Each now sat on his bed and prayed in silence, for today would be his last day on earth and tonight he would sup in paradise.
*9:30 a.m, United States Central Command Office of*

25

*Electronic Counter Surveillance, McDill Air Force Base, Tampa, Florida*

"Diesirae631 back on line, 11:45 hours Zulu time. Message: "Four hours, Sword One, Four and a Half Hours, Sword Two. Allahu Akbar."

Tech sergeant Quentin Younger, sipping his third cup of coffee of the morning, sat up in his chair and gazed at the screen. The endless scrolling of data which, on occasion, would suddenly highlight a tweet and color-code it for level of concern and need to report. This one was coming up red-flagged, meaning it needed a human review and not just a computerized review. It was a message plucked out of the hundreds of millions of monitored tweets flooding the world every hour.

Quentin scanned the identifying information attachment to the message. It was an account set up nearly a year ago, some innocuous text messages back and forth, the last one a complaint about a lost bet regarding the World Cup. World Cup tweets were drawing some notice when originating out of Syria as coded messages, but there had been silence on the account since the games had ended.

Someone up the food chain had pegged diesirae631 as a source of concern. He punched in a query to trace the followers. Several dozen were in Syria; there was talk several months back about the games and one complaint about a failed encounter with a Belgian woman working in a medical aid station. Curious… there were new followers in the States as of this morning, all with hashtags of diesirae with higher numbers. No responses though. He checked those points of reception: all were accounts that were activated within the last two weeks, purchased as cheap convenience store phones. Very curious.

It was coming up on break time and he yawned.

Another curious item cropped up. Someone had code-named the surveillance file for this account as Dies irae. What the heck?

He punched in a Google search on the term. What was it, French, Spanish? Nothing significant. He scanned the line of possible alternatives. Dies irae was the third item, a Wikipedia article. Strange, something called a Gregorian chant. Latin. "Day of Wrath," a hymn from the thirteenth century that became associated with the Great Plague of the fourteenth century.

Great Plague? He had some memory of a high school history teacher talking about that.

It was break time; the coffee had worked through him and he needed to go. Creepy stuff. Why would someone in Syria be sending messages around in Latin? They hated anything to do with that language, still cursing the Crusaders of a thousand years ago as their excuse to commit murder today. Regardless, the hashtag was coded as a high priority and he hit the send button to circulate a message received, warning that it was being followed by receivers within the States, and therefore would be bounced to NSA for further review. His job done, he got up for the restroom and silently cursed his hangover.

*10:30 a.m., the White House*

Dale Hinman took a second look at his screen, not sure if he was actually seeing it for real. "Dies Irae." He didn't know what it really meant other than the fact that he was to kick the word up to the very top. He attached the email that was sent up from the NSA and forwarded it a very short physical distance, to the center of this very building.

Something was about to happen. The message was time-stamped 7:45 a.m. today. Whatever it was, Sword One would start at 11:45. He had done his job; let those down the hall in the Oval Office complex figure out what was next.

# CHAPTER THREE

*11:10 a.m., near Portland, Maine*

Shelly was down for her morning nap, thank God. Wendy had been such an easy child, Kathy thought as she carefully closed the door to the nursery, or was it that she was now thirty-seven and no longer a new wide-eyed mom of twenty-five and still fascinated by every single thing her darling did?

The news was on in the kitchen. More about the shooting in Syracuse. A video surveillance tape had just been released; the police alerted this morning by a hotel manager, who, seeing the gunman's image from the school's security camera had scrolled his own tape back and come up with a frightening match. The camera in the hotel was of the man leaving a back exit and it was time-stamped only twenty minutes before the killings at the school. But what was far more disturbing now was the fact that less than thirty minutes after the incident hit the news in Syracuse, five men, obviously Middle Eastern, had walked out the back door of the same hotel, gotten into a single car, and disappeared. One of them had shared the room with the gunman.

All schools in Syracuse were closed for the day and the city resembled Boston after the bombing of the marathon race, going into a full lockdown with every local and county officer in a manhunt along with a national guard military police unit being called in as well as federal officials. The hotel video provided at least a black and white image of the car that the other five had left in, but no license plate number. Syracuse was in a state of panic. An impromptu rally of angry parents was ramping up in front of one of the closed schools, denouncing the school system for inadequate security due to the failure to provide new security locks on classroom doors that would bolt the doors shut. A parent speaking for the group, demanding the new bullet proof steel security doors, was standing outside the glass window of the typical one story middle school building that stretched for a hundred yards.

The fact that the lone shooter was stopped in the first minute of his attack by an off-duty police officer who had come to the school early to pick up his son who was ill, did draw some notice and comment and the officer was posthumously hailed as a hero. No one had noted nor emphasized the point that it was an armed parent, already in the school parking lot, who by lucky chance was there to stop the tragedy from becoming far worse.

Kathy finally launched into loading up the dishwasher while the news shifted to the death of some reality show star. Disgusted, she clicked the volume down and logged onto her Facebook page to upload photos of Shelly's first birthday party from the weekend. Why was it the kid just loved to smear food, especially anything with chocolate, all over her face and hair and then just sit there laughing as she and Bob groaned with disgust? Cute photos though.

Some new posts were there: friends from college and her own teaching days were discussing the incident in Syracuse. When Bob had told her of his decision several years ago to ignore all the rules and carry a concealed weapon, they had agreed it was wise to avoid any comment whatsoever on the issue on any social media and in any conversation that stood the remotest chance of being overheard, especially by Wendy who had the typical loud mouth of a twelve-year-old. One never knew when the bounce back might hit. A post could be reposted in self-righteous angst about protecting "our children," and then forwarded to Bob's principal with the demand that he be "checked out."

The usual argument was raging between her friends. Mary Browning, her college roommate down in Austin, was in a fury over the entire ongoing immigrant crisis and was now upset over the killing of the three border patrol officers just south of where she lived. Another friend replied that Syracuse was proof that more trained security officers were needed in every school in the country.

A tweet from Mary popped up on Kathy's pad: "Just heard lots of sirens on Interstate 35." Kathy looked up to the television on the kitchen counter. There was a helicopter hovering above a highway near downtown Austin and a line of police cars. A high-speed chase was in progress and she saw the caption read, "Shooting in Austin suburb."

She turned the sound back up.

"We have live video now from our affiliate in Austin. Police are in a high-speed pursuit on Interstate 35, just north of the state highway 290 interchange."

There was no commentary for a moment; someone in the New York studio gasped that it looked like gunfire coming from the vehicle being pursued. It sped past a tractor-trailer, which suddenly jackknifed across the highway, taking out thc lcad policc car.

"This is bad, it's bad!" someone cried off camera, "It looks like puffs of smoke or something impacting that red car heading southbound… oh no, no…!'"

A southbound car, traveling in the direction opposite the vehicle being pursued, veered off the highway and rolled up onto its side as it slammed into the guardrail. The helicopter camera focused on that crash for a moment, then swung back to the jackknifed truck, a police car tangled in the wreckage. Some of the pursuing vehicles were stopping, others were climbing up around the shoulder and accelerating to continue the chase.

"There is definite gunfire coming from that vehicle!" It was the morning anchor speaking in a small box to one side of the screen. "You can see the puffs of smoke. There! They've hit another car, that white SUV. My God, it looks like automatic fire; they've shredded that car!"

Kathy looked at the clock, it was 11:30. Bob should be on lunch break by now. The news in Syracuse and now this? It made her feel uneasy as she picked up her pad.

"You seeing the news?" she texted to Bob.

*11:32 a.m., Chamberlain Middle School near Portland, Maine*

As he walked into the faculty lounge his cell phone beeped, it was a message from Kathy. Bob put his lunch bag down on a table in order to pull out his phone and check it. He refused to keep his lunch in the faculty fridge; it was gross. The last time he looked, a bulging Tupperware container was ready to explode. Ed Winston, the eighth grade science teacher, said it was an experiment and if not, a hazmat team should be called in, but no one was volunteering to clean it out.

He paused to look up at the small television in the stuffy and rather ill-kept faculty lounge. No one spoke; the television was always tuned at this time of day to an inane talk show, not as bad as the one that always wound up in fist fights, but nearly as bad. He checked Kathy's text. It wasn't the usual "Love you" message or a report of some antic or complaint about Shelly.

"Hey, can we switch the channel?" he asked, looking up at the screen. Two of the male faculty, bent over their lunches, silently nodded agreement but kept their heads down, saying nothing. Margaret Redding, as usual, held court here and few dared to cross her. To interfere with her favorite program was cause for a war which she always won. Years ago other faculty who shared the same break time had given up arguing. There was always the incvitablc accusation later of inappropriate language, demeaning looks and attitude, or an offense that hinted at heinous crimes, that would have to be dragged before the principal for arbitration or bumped up to the personnel office for the district. It was more hassle than it was worth and never a victory, only another humiliation or, at best, a suggestion that the faculty form yet another committee to decide what should be on the television at which time. Of course Margaret made sure that she ran that committee and that her show stayed on.

"You know I prefer this program," Margaret replied coolly, without even bothering to look at Bob.

Without bothering to ask permission he boldly walked toward the TV, looking for the remote control. He made eye contact with Margaret. The remote was resting on the lunch table, directly in front of her, and if he reached for it, there would be another "incident."

"Margaret, I'm getting text messages from my wife that there's some breaking news. Let's switch the channel."

No eye contact, only one word: "No."

Bitch. Of course he didn't say that out loud.

He stared at the two other faculty in the room for support. Both of the men kept their heads down, ignoring the entire exchange.

He touched his phone to an internet search and started to type in the address to one of the local stations.

"Bob, you know policy is that the faculty lounge is a computer-free zone during lunch hours," Margaret announced as she picked up the remote and made a show of turning up the volume on the television.

33

The program showed several women sitting around a coffee table, voices raised in heated argument about whether a popular male star should divorce his cheating wife. She had been caught on a cell phone camera swimming nude and making out with another female star on a movie set in the Mediterranean. The video had been playing over and over on numerous websites for the last day. One of the commentators giggled slyly and suggested that of course her husband would welcome both of them back.

He ignored Margaret and the asinine television belching out its mindless drivel, and held his phone close to try and read a scrolling text across the bottom of the tiny screen: something about the incident in Austin. It was impossible to see and his frustration was growing. He looked back at Margaret who was putting the remote down so she could take another bite from her sandwich.

Bob leaned across the table and snatched it. He turned, and, to add insult to her injury, selected the local Fox station which he knew she detested. She exploded with fury, accusations, and then threats...

*11:35 a.m., Portland, Maine*

The five gathered in one hotel room. The weather was cool enough that their long jackets did not look too out of place, but once into their vehicles, the jackets would come off. All were wearing full tactical gear: black webbing with chest pockets holding extra magazines of 9mm hollow points. Kevlar vests were underneath the webbing, protecting them from neck to crotch from anything less than a heavy jacketed armor-piercing round. They would leave in two vehicles, one a standard size American-made car rented the day before by their handler from an agency near the airport. Three would go to their target in that

34

vehicle. The other three would remain in the Tahoe and drive the quarter mile to a nearby fast food restaurant, park in the back, and wait out the final minutes.

The prayer for those about to become martyrs was short; the five faced to the east-southeast. One of them had placed a small mark with a grease pen on the wall so that they were properly looking toward Mecca.

That was all, no cries out loud and no chants; that had been done for them the night before they left Syria. The few weeks of indulging in the decadence of their enemies had been merely a diversion without any stain of sin, for those who were to become holy martyrs, all sin would be washed away in the blood of their death as the prophet had promised them.

There would be no pity now. The playacting of smiling at a child and commenting how cute he was when the toddler had grinned at one of them while they waited in line for a meal, was over now. If any had inwardly blanched at the thought of what they would unleash in little more than fifteen minutes, they had been liberated of that conscience by participating in the spring offensive into Iraq. Each of them had been required to participate in the executions after villages and Mosul were seized. All had been singled out for a few days of training and practice on targets in a Christian neighborhood. The targets ranged from silent grandmothers who prayed as they awaited their fate to screaming mothers begging for mercy to children younger than the smiling toddler in the restaurant awaiting a meal with a toy. Their actions in Mosul had been enough to desensitize them to any aspect of their mission. Their leader had lavished praise upon them and promised the paradise that awaited them.

Their handler, who had infiltrated America more than a year ago, tapped on the door, signaling that the vehicles were ready and waiting. The five left the room, just a few feet from the side exit. An Hispanic maid saw them advancing down the corridor and started to smile a greeting, but something about their demeanor caused her to back against the wall and stare at them warily as they passed.

She knew without doubt that she saw with them the shadow of death passing by, a shadow that her grandmother had often spoken of when she was a child. She made the sign of the cross as they went out the door, then hurried to find the manager, driven by an instinct that something was not right with these men who had kept their room chained and barred during the two days they had stayed as guests, refusing entry even to have their beds made.

Three heavy canisters were in the back of the black late-model Tahoe. They popped the back hatch and shifted the canisters to the back seat of the smaller American car. The canisters contained six shoulder weapons: three primary weapons of .223 and three backup weapons of personal choice. Two had requested 12-gauge pumps, easily altered to hold six rounds with a mix of anti-personnel and heavier "pumpkin ball" ammunition for breaking down a door lock. The third preferred a short .45 semi auto carbine that could be easily slung over the shoulder.

The heaviest part of the burden being transferred was the thousand rounds of ammunition for each of their primary weapons, already loaded into thirty round magazines. Packed under the seats of the Tahoe were several thousand more rounds for the ubiquitous AK-47s for the second team, who would stay in the Tahoe. They were the "Sword Two" team who would begin their attack a half hour after their brothers of "Sword One" attacked.

No explosives were with their "packages." The wise evaluation of their leader was that there was too much risk in acquiring and moving explosives. This decision had been argued; it was easy enough to buy black powder on the open market, or, with a bit of training, learn how to convert a few bags of lawn fertilizer into explosives. The caliph, however, replied that such a move would be a tip-off and vetoed it with the strictest orders to not attempt any such purchases once in the heartland of the infidels.

But it was easy and even amusing to assemble a couple of dozen small boxes that looked like IEDs during their final hours of waiting, boxes to scatter in the wake of their assaults and slow to a crawl any response by the infidels sent against them.

They moved the shipping canisters into the second vehicle, drew the weapons and laid them into the rear of the vehicle for quick access, and readied the satchels for hauling the dozens of magazines of ammunition and fake IEDs, to be instantly grabbed the moment they reached their target. They started to climb into the two cars.

"Excuse me sirs, are you checking out?"

They looked up. It was the hotel manager coming out the back exit behind them. He looked Indian or Pakistani, his accent a giveaway. Slender, dark skinned, he was all smiles but obviously nervous. They had seen him looking more than once in their direction as they ate dinner the evening before in the hotel's small restaurant and bar.

They had indeed aroused some instinct in him. He wasn't Hindu; he was a Pakistani Christian who had fled the region near the Afghan border with his family back in the early 1990s. He had raised his children as Americans and was grateful every day for the peace of this land. The sight of these men triggered some instinct of fear. It was their eyes. As a young man he remembered fighters

37

coming across the border during the Soviet war in Afghanistan, recruits flooding into the war zone from Saudi Arabia, Jordan, and Syria to become jihadists and kill communists, but happy to kill Christians as well even though the local Christian community ran a hospital for wounded refugees. These fighters had the same dead, shark-like eyes.

The way one of them turned and faced him told him that even here, in America, in the state of Maine, which all assumed was far safer than places like New York or Chicago, was now as dangerous as the streets of his home village, as dangerous as Mosul, Tikrit and Aleppo. It was the last thought of his life. Though nervous at approaching the men, they did not even give him time for that nervousness to turn to fear.

Little more than three seconds after he asked the question his brain was shattered by the impact of a single round to his forehead, his conscious thoughts did not even register the flash from the muzzle of the 9mm fired from less than three feet away, nor did he hear the triumphal cry of "Allahu akbar!"

The two vehicles left the parking lot thirty seconds later. The maid, who had apprehensively stood in the doorway and watched as her friend and manager innocently walked into his death, collapsed to her knees, screaming and calling out to the Blessed Virgin, while another maid, a refugee from the madness of Ethiopia who was far more used to the sight of cold blooded killings, began to fumble a call to 911.

# CHAPTER FOUR

*11:43 a.m., near Portland, Maine*

Kathy looked up from her pad. She had been trying to connect to her friend Mary in Austin, Texas, texting her, while her attention remained glued to the television where the murders along Interstate 35 near Mary's neighborhood were continuing and the ticker along the bottom of the television reported a second shooting incident in Syracuse. Apparently an accomplice of yesterday's school shooter had been cornered in the parking lot of a shopping mall.

Kathy heard a siren, a police car racing past on the state highway, one block over from her home. Seconds later a second police car followed.

It sent a chill down her spine. What was going on?

A third police car, seconds later.

Fear. Her heart constricted, beating faster. Surely this was not all interrelated in some way? She and Bob had shared whispered conversations often enough after Wendy was asleep as to the possibility that some horror could indeed happen here and what was their drill, their response? They had talked about it scores of times but were those fears and whispered conversations now triggering her into an overreaction?

She texted Bob again, "Turn on the news now!" He had not responded so far.

*11:44 a.m., Joshua Chamberlain Middle School, Portland, Maine*

He had made the mistake of setting the remote control back down on the table, a gesture of long habit when watching a program with Kathy who on their second date had accused him of being a typical male because he

39

hogged the television remote control.

Margaret Redding snatched it back, switched the channel back to the program she had been watching, clutched the remote and glared at him defiantly, all but begging him to try and make a physical grab for it. She had already announced that she was filing a complaint of harassment, that to even try and touch her to get the remote would be a career-ender for certain and she was egging him on to do so. There was a flicker of a smile of the self-righteous professional victim who sensed that she just might have one hell of an excellent case if she could push him just one step further. At the very least, in a few more minutes she would waddle out of the lounge, crying, head to the principal's office and then take the rest of the day off due to the fear and anxiety he had created by his aggressive, dominant behavior.

"What the hell?" It was Vince Rossingnol, the quiet, introspective English literature teacher, who, as always, studiously avoided involvement in any confrontation with Margaret.

Bob thought Vince was standing up and stepping in at last to the confrontation with the "tyrant," as all whispered when she was not present, of the faculty lounge. It'd be a two-to-one vote as to who controlled the television and a witness that he had not physically touched Margaret. Vince standing up might be a crucial point to argue after school when, yet again, he was summoned to the office to answer Margaret's accusations.

But Vince was not facing them at all; he was at the window, splitting open a couple of the dust-covered blinds and looking out to the front of the school. A blue sedan had pulled up directly by the walkway entrance, in a no parking or standing zone. Three men were piling out, dressed in black, reaching into the back seats, and pulling out satchels to sling over their shoulders. One of them stood straight up. He was holding a rifle aloft in one hand.

"What in hell are those sons of bitches doing?" Vince cried, his voice rising and cracking.

Margaret turned her wrath away from Bob to begin chiding Vince for his inappropriate use of language on school grounds, a definite violation as well, then went silent.

"Are those guns? They aren't allowed to do that!" she cried.

Bob turned away from the television to look out the window.

"Merciful God in heaven, it's happening!" he gasped.

The three men rushed toward the front entrance. The way the wing of the main building was angled toward the parking lot and main entrance, Bob could see the front entrance, which was less than a hundred feet away.

Charlie, their elderly security and resource officer, was actually exiting the front door, his only weapon a taser and pepper spray, both of them still latched and buttoned securely to his belt.

In these first seconds Bob simply could not react. Though the analogy was something from before his time, he remembered reading how some folks described such a moment of frightful shock as being like an old record that kept skipping and playing the same line over and over: this can't be real, this can't be real, this can't be real...

It became very real when the leader of the group slowed, raised a pistol and calmly put a 9mm hollow point bullet into Charlie's head from twenty feet away, the old man collapsing like a broken doll.

"Jesus Christ this is it!" Bob cried but it took several seconds for him to reach into his pocket for his Ruger.

Margaret started to scream, backing up against the

wall, ironically still clutching the television remote control. Vince turned back from the window, gasping, and began to sag against the window frame, sobbing, already in a state of shock at the sight of the back of Charlie's head exploding from the impact of the round.

Bob had played this scenario out in his mind hundreds of times. Nearly every day that he walked down the corridor to his office and classroom area he'd ask himself, "What do I do if...? What do I do?" But he had never played this one out in his mind: What do I do if I am in the faculty lounge, it's lunchtime and not one, but three, gunmen storm the building, burdened down with multiple weapons, and blow the brains out of our kind, elderly security guard on the front lawn of the school as their opening move?

Thoughts started to race and his mind, on the edge of panic, finally latched onto one: Where is Wendy? Is she already in the lunch room, or is it math class? God, what time is it? Where is she? Where is my daughter?

A bell started to ring, loud, insistent, piercing. Was it the lunch bell, or the alert for lockdown?

Now a flurry of shots thundered down the hallway. Screams. Margaret turned and actually managed to lock the door to the faculty lounge.

"Get away from the door!" Bob commanded, holding his pistol up and chambering a round, but still not sure where to go.

Margaret's gaze fixed on the small pistol in his right hand. More gunfire sounded from down the corridor, echoing like firecrackers. Screaming, more screaming, *children's* screams.

"You can't have a gun, Petersen. I'll report you for this!"

"Shut the hell up, bitch and clear the door!" he

snapped, grabbing her by the shoulder and shoving her bulky frame to one side. He unlocked the door and opened it. Whatever instincts were still working for him, he knew he had to do something, at least for his daughter.

He took a deep breath. At last some flash of clarity settled in. His instincts as a father and a protector overrode everything else.

He stepped into the corridor. The alarm for lockdown was sounding, reverberating, making it hard to think. On the far side of the main office complex was the wing for the gym, dining hall, library, science labs, his own IT office, and more classrooms. Behind him doors to classrooms were opening up. In spite of the drills held at the start of the year before the students arrived, a fair number of teachers were reacting in the opening moments with curiosity rather than as they had been trained to do.

Surely this could not be real? they were asking themselves and each other. A mistake? Bob heard someone shouting that question. Was this all a mistake or for real? Another shouted that some damn idiot of an administrator had gone over the edge and decided to pull an actual "real" drill with firecrackers included. If so, heads would roll after this one.

Bob glanced back in the opposite direction of the gunfire. Where was Wendy's fourth period classroom? Was she in the lunch room or still in math? The door to her math classroom was a few feet down the corridor and across from the faculty lunch room. The door was closed, lights off. My God, had they gone for lunch and she was on the other side of the building with the murderers between him and his daughter?

Suddenly an explosion of shots rang out and glass shattered. He whipped his head around toward the office complex and saw the large glass window of the front office break apart, broken glass cascading down, screams coming from within.

He caught a glimpse of the principal, Mr. Carl, gentle soul, who insisted on wearing a bow-tie which Bob thought made him look rather nerdy. Kids might say behind his back that he was somewhat "dorky" but they all knew he had a loving heart. He was stepping out into the junction of the main corridor with the office complex.

How many times had Bob argued about this moment, what to do if a gunman hit their school? Carl always replied that they would follow policy as they had been trained to do. According to his training, Carl was to be in his office calling the police and sounding the alarm. But he must have been down in the lunch room.

A group of children appeared at the end of the hallway, a class that had been heading to the lunch room, and in those first seconds their teacher turned them back. Carl shouted for them to run for their classroom. A split second later several bullets exited his back and he sagged. The man was using his body to shield the terrified children even as he died. The group was running toward Bob. More shots resounded.

God in heaven, it was Wendy's class! They were being led by their teacher Patty Carlson, a first-year teacher, still fired up with idealism about her profession. But there was no three-credit course at the state university to train her for this moment; all of the other courses she had been required to take were now meaningless.

There was much he had to process in the next few seconds. Carl was down, several children he had tried to shield were collapsing. Was that Wendy? The bright pink designer scarf she was so proud of, a birthday present from her mother, was around her neck. The scarf made her stand out and it filled him with terror that it would draw the attention of the killers as well. She was at the back of the line of panicked children running toward him. He saw a dark form at the end of the corridor, bulky, dressed in black. The man's shoulder weapon was raised. He aimed straight at the backs of the fleeing children.

Flashes, an explosion of rounds. Children at the end of the fleeing group dropped, one after the other, shot in the back. There was an instant of silence, then the sound of a magazine dropping.

I should charge him and shoot, the thought screamed at him. An instructor, when he took training, talked about "muscle memory": of learning to react by instinct. The horror and confusion of it all was so overwhelming that he simply had not raised his pistol yet, all attention was focused on Wendy as he instinctively started toward her to pull her to safety, wherever that might be.

He caught a glimpse of Wendy. She was down, but then coming back up, knocked over by the child directly behind her who had been shot. Her math teacher turned back to grab her, shepherding her children, physically placing herself at the end of the line to shield them, pushing them toward her classroom.

The gunman slapped another magazine in, started to aim it down the corridor and then, as if distracted, turned to his left, and popped round after round at a range of but a few feet into a terrified group of children who were streaming out of the gym, trying to flee to their classrooms for lockdown as their teacher had trained them to do.

Wendy was up, shoved forward by Patty. Bob grabbed her by the arm, placing his body between her and the killer before the gunman's attention returned to them, and together they bolted into the perceived safety of her classroom, slamming the door shut behind them and locking it.

More shots rang out in the hallway, then screaming, then a distinctive cry, "Allahu akbar, Allahu akbar, Allahu akbar!" and that focused Bob at last.

This was not some random shooting, some cowardly son-of-a-bitch lone shooter, or even a team of two or three psychotics. With their triumphal cries he knew with absolute certainty that this was not the lone, crazed, sick shooter of the American scenario, the American nightmare ever since Columbine. It was Russia, 2004. This was the Chechnya scenario, the Beslan school massacre of 2004. The worst nightmare of all his nightmares as a teacher.

The Beslan school massacre in the southern Russia province of Chechnya, was a deliberately designed mass murder, the perfect storm of a terrorist mentality that viewed infidel children as tools to terrorize the enemy before sending all of them to hell.

A handful of Islamic murderers who claimed they were fighters for an independent state seized the school in the Russian province on the first day of classes, which by Russian tradition was a time of celebration, proud parents taking their children to school and bringing small gifts of flowers and fruit to the teachers. But rather than a school opening with ceremonies and children singing traditional folk and patriotic songs, the day began with armed terrorists storming and seizing control of the building.

First they herded the male teachers and older male students to a back room and systematically cut their throats to eliminate any chance of resistance.

It was an attack designed to terrorize a nation and the next step transcended anything even the Nazis had done to cower a population. Girls as young as ten were dragged to the roof of the building, over which news helicopters were hovering and reporting on the attack. Several terrorists held a child down as one of their fellow "freedom fighters"

46

raped the child and then while raping her, cut her throat. The Russian government, which still controlled its mass media, immediately shut the media links down with the concern that, whether it was right or wrong, the sight of this depravity might trigger a frenzied counter-response. The intent of the terrorists was to arouse a religious war between Orthodox and Muslim, and to instill panic across the entire nation.

Children caught up as pawns in that nightmare hell were then herded into a gym for what became a standoff of several days. The hostages were trapped in sweltering heat with no food or water so that many turned to drinking their own urine to slake their thirst. In the final conclusion of the horror, when security forces stormed the building, the terrorists, with a final cry of Allahu akbar, detonated explosives ringing the roof of the gym, collapsing the structure. Over three hundred innocent victims died.

It was a nightmare scenario that had lingered with Bob across the years. He had warned of it, and with the shouts of triumph out in the hallway, he knew it had indeed come to his school outside of Portland, Maine.

He scanned the classroom. Children were sobbing, one girl was screaming hysterically, cradling a shattered arm as a young boy, who seemed so calm, was wrapping a belt around her upper arm to make a tourniquet. A kid with some boy scout training, he thought.

Another explosion of shots, rapid fire, echoed and there was more screaming out in the hallway. He looked about, still clutching Wendy to his side. The Ruger was in his right hand, still unused. Six shots of a lightweight pistol against what they were carrying? It might have worked against some damn crazed bastard like the one who had shot up the school in Connecticut, but now?

There was more gunfire; the main lights in the hallway

flickered off, a fire alarm began to shriek, and seconds later sprinklers in the hallway came on. Emergency lights switched on and flashed, adding to the terror and confusion.

Clear, clear your thoughts, he kept repeating to himself.

A glimpse out the window of the classroom door revealed a child lying in the hallway, twitching spasmodically. Another child started to get up and then the back of her head just exploded.

"God in heaven, where are You?" he cried.

More shots went off in the corridor; it sounded like one of the killers was coming closer. He stepped away from the door, checking the room.

The windows. The classroom faced west to the open playing yard and ball field. There were children out there in gym clothes, a teacher, one of the coaches, herding them together. *God, don't bring them back in, run the other way!*

He went to a window. The upper part was standard safety glass and a small hand crank controlled a lower window that could not open more than a foot wide.

More gunfire reverberated in the hallway, then screams. The gunfire sounded as if it were receding, then was followed by a long rapid burst. My God, they're beginning to move room to room!

The decision was near instant.

"Out the windows!" he shouted.

Patty, standing in the corner, surrounded by nearly a score of trembling children stared at him wide-eyed.

"We're supposed to lie down, Bob."

"Out, get out!" he screamed, trying to pick Wendy up with one arm and force her into the narrow escape of the crank-opened window. She was kicking in panic, refusing.

He pulled her back, set her down, pocketed the pistol, then picked up a student desk and slammed it against the plate glass window. It recoiled back in his hand but the window cracked. The children flinched.

"Damn it, break!"

He hit it again, slamming the desk in, and the window finally shattered, safety glass breaking apart, a few fragments still clinging to the frame.

Wendy ran to him and clung to his neck.

"Wendy, get out and run! Run and don't stop. Don't look back, just run for the woods over there on the far side of the field!"

"Daddy?"

"Go!"

He struggled to break her grasp around his neck and then to his horror saw that the coach out in the field, with safety only a hundred yards away, had actually rounded his students up into a group and was standing in the play yard, hesitating, looking toward the building as if some part of it would still give safety. A long burst of fire erupted, and the children outside began to drop. The group broke apart, running in panic. As they scattered, several ran to the parking lot but were cut down, collapsing into small bloody heaps. One tried to get up and was hit yet again, the shot demonstrating the utter lack of mercy. Wendy saw it all, twisting, writhing to get out of his grip, screaming that she did not want to go outside.

The months of training were now making it all so easy for the holy warriors of the caliph. Two were to first hit the main entrance, kill the staff in the central office area and any ridiculous security man who might have a pistol locked away in his office. One of the two would then hold the entrance while the second covered the back entry, shooting down any who tried to flee that way, and keeping their prey pent up in the building. The emergency exits out of the gym and dining hall were then easily blocked by hanging several fake IEDs on the doors and announcing that as long as they stayed put, no one would be hurt. That if any tried to open the doors, they would all be blown apart.

The third would then methodically begin to work his way down the two main classroom corridors, the wings of the building that contained five hundred and thirty-eight students and thirty-seven staff and teachers. Once the classrooms were wiped out, attention would then be focused on those cowering in the gym and dining hall for the second stage of their plan.

All of the information they needed in laying out the plan for this school had been garnered from the school district's website, from photographs of the interior posted by students, by a new math teacher proudly showing off her classroom, and by photographs and video clips of school plays, festivals, and sporting events. How these Americans loved to film and post their children's sporting events and provide so many details for a trained eye planning to kill them all! There were even blueprints and photographs of the newly-built classrooms from sixteen years ago, showing the design and layout of their new school.

After seizing the main office complex they knocked out the electricity and activated the fire alarms, setting off sprinklers to add to the confusion.

With that done, the work now commenced of moving from classroom to classroom.

A local police car pulled up to the curb in less than four minutes, summoned by the frightened call of the principal's secretary, who did as she was drilled to do: get that call out immediately. And then she died.

The officer clambered out of his vehicle and saw old Charlie sprawled out on the walkway. There had been intense debate in the years since Columbine, renewed after Newtown, as to how the first officer on the scene of a school shooting should react. Wait for backup or charge straight in? The argument had shifted to rushing the building, since most of the killers, at the sight of a police officer, often shot themselves and ended the madness. The local police chief told his personnel that they'd have to make their best judgment call when they arrived on the scene. As for himself, if he knew children were about to die at the hands of some damn lunatic, he would go in and to hell with waiting for backup. Every second meant a life saved or lost.

So the first officer there, hearing the gunshots and screaming, knew he had to go in. The call from the secretary had not been clear, just a scream that there was a "shooter in the building," then the sound of gunfire was followed by the signal cutting off and the near-hysterical 911 dispatcher shouting the news onto the police circuit. So he moved forward, the jihadist waiting for him chuckling at how amateurish the man was. The jihadist switched his weapon from full auto to single shot and put a well-aimed round into the man's head, dropping him next to the foolish old security guard.

The sight of the two dead bodies would give the next approaching officer reason to pause. In order for the plan to work well, to achieve all that they wished to achieve, they needed the next hour free of interference.

The leader of the three holy warriors clicked on the phone he was carrying, no more need for security regarding that, selected the website to the local news station, and smiled as he saw that their regular programming had been interrupted. They were already reporting "an incident that appears to be unfolding at Joshua Chamberlain Middle School." It truly was going according to plan.

Bob clutched Wendy, watching as the children outside scattered across the playground area, while out in the hallway he could clearly hear the gunfire erupting in a classroom across the corridor and one doorway down from the faculty lounge area.

He heard loud screams, prayers, begging, relentless shooting, and repeated cries of "Allahu akbar!"

If they were following a pattern, this room would be next. He hugged Wendy fiercely and kissed her on the cheek.

"Wendy, you've got to run. You've got to run as fast as you've ever run. Go to the woods across the field. Now run!"

He tried to force her slender body through the shattered window. She began to kick and struggle, slicing her knee open on the edge of the shattered glass in the window frame.

"Daddy, no! I want to stay with you."

He forcefully pulled her loose from her deathlike grip around his neck.

"I love you. Tell Mommy and Shelly I love them. Now RUN!"

He threw her out the window so that she landed sprawling, scrambling to her hands and knees, sobbing, a look on her face as if he had brutally rejected her. She actually started to try to climb back in.

"Damn you Wendy! Listen to me! I am ordering you to run. Do it!"

He tried to force an angry gaze as if furious with her,

to frighten her even more than the horror of what was around her. She looked at him, shocked, and stepped back, then winced as the sound of gunfire echoed around her.

"Run!"

She turned away and finally began to stagger across the play yard.

"I love you, sweetie," he whispered, then turned back to face the others in the room.

"Patty, listen to me, we've got to get all these kids out."

"Bob, we shouldn't. We can't." Her face was stunned at what she had just witnessed.

"Damn it Patty, do it!"

"Bob, we're not supposed to."

She was in shock, beyond the ability to reason and crucial seconds were ticking by as brutal death approached.

He glanced around the room, saw the boy who had struggled to put a tourniquet on his bleeding classmate.

"Your name, son?"

"Johnnie O'Sullivan."

"You a boy scout?"

More gunfire out in the hallway, then the sound in the distance of a siren, at last.

"Yes sir."

"Son, I want you to run, tell the police there are three gunmen. They are Muslim terrorists most likely armed with automatic weapons who plan to kill everyone inside. You got that?"

Before the boy could make a reply, Bob picked him up and unceremoniously dumped him out the window.

Then the gunfire hit the door of the classroom, the rounds easily piercing it. More screaming, a child in the middle of the room was cut down.

He stepped up against the wall alongside the doorway,

drawing his weapon back out, trying to remember if he had chambered a round in the semi-auto he was holding. He pulled the slider back and an unfired bullet popped out. Damn it! He had chambered a round but in the confusion forgotten he had done so. A damn amateur move. The bullet, one of only six rounds in his possession, rolled across the floor. Damn it, pick it up later; you've only got five left. He waited for the door to swing open…

*Near Portland, Maine*

"My God, oh my God!"

Kathy Petersen stood transfixed, watching the local news feed.

"We repeat, there are reports of a shooting incident unfolding at Chamberlain Middle School. Our eyecam helicopter is racing to the scene and should be there any moment."

The video feed from the helicopter was on, focused forward as the pilot swung northeastward, flying parallel to I-95. The highway was filled with police cars responding to the terrified calls coming in from the school.

"We also now have a confirmed report of a fatal shooting at a hotel by the Falmouth exit that may be related.

"This appears to be a frightful tragedy unfolding just outside of Portland, Maine."

The reporter paused, touching her earpiece, nodding.

"As soon as we have a helicopter over Chamberlain Middle School we will come back on but we now have this urgent news release from our main studio in New York."

The image shifted, but Kathy was no longer watching it. She was running into Shelly's room to rouse her from her nap.

"A tragedy of national proportions appears to be

54

unfolding across America at this moment," the report echoed from the kitchen television. "We now have confirmed reports of three schools: one near Austin, a second in Bakersfield California, and a third near Portland Maine, that appear to be under attack. In a minute or so we should have a live helicopter feed from the school in Maine."

She had Shelly out of her crib, the toddler fussing to be woken up so rudely, and, feeling her mother's panic, started to cry. Kathy wasn't sure what to do, but to stay here was not the answer. She returned to the kitchen. Holding Shelly, she used her free hand to call Bob. His laughing voice came on "Hey, busy at the moment, but leave a message and someday I'll get back to you!"

"Bob, find Wendy and get the hell out of there now!" she screamed. She hung up, attention focused back to the television report.

"Just a moment, just a moment... we are getting a fourth report now from our affiliate in Charlotte, North Carolina, of an elementary school in Hickory, North Carolina: numerous gun shots, a police officer dead in front of the school."

The reporter in the New York studio turned her gaze from the camera, the steady professional composure of a national level news anchor shattered as she turned to look off camera.

"Everyone in this studio, shut the hell up!" she yelled. "I want accurate reports only. I only want accurate reports coming out of here, now do your jobs!"

The reporter looked back to the camera, obviously shaken.

"My apologies, we are trying to sort this out as it comes in and to avoid panic."

A second reporter came on camera, a popular anchor

of the station's mid-afternoon news program, sitting down beside her and trying to appear calm. She gratefully acknowledged his presence. He was well known for having been a reporter who had gone in with the troops in the 2003 campaign into Iraq and had repeatedly been under fire. He deferentially held up a sheet of paper, offering to hand it to her, but she nodded for him to read the report.

"I've just been handed a copy of a report from our affiliate station in Billings, Montana, and I quote, "A siege is unfolding at an elementary school in the northwest section of that city. There appears to be a coordinated attack now underway against at least five of our nation's elementary and middle schools. It is obviously a terrorist attack on our nation's children. We promise to keep you abreast as the situation unfolds.

"We now have a feed from our affiliate in Portland with a news helicopter over…" he looked down at a note someone had handed to him, "…Chamberlain Middle School."

The few seconds that she took to watch triggered a sob of pure horror in Kathy. It was an aerial shot of the playground! The playground where Wendy took recess every day when the weather was good, a place of swings, of slides, and of monkey bars, where in winter snowball fights were forbidden but broke out anyway.

"Oh God, Wendy, my baby," Kathy gasped.

The playground now looked like a war zone, which in fact it was. The camera swung across half a dozen small bodies sprawled in the yard, revealing red splotches, pools of blood, children crawling, a teacher crouching low and carrying a child. And then live, for all the nation to see, the teacher went limp, a puff, a mist of blood and clothing burst out of him, both he and the child going down. The

56

camera began to zoom in but then pulled back, as if it were too horrific to be seen. The reaction was almost instinctive to not gaze too closely upon the horror, in the same way that cameras were finally turned away on 9/11 when, by the hundreds, bodies plunged down the faces of the north and south towers of the World Trade Center. But this time it was children who were dying.

Kathy's phone rang. Bob! She almost dropped Shelly who was kicking and squirming, while sliding the screen of the phone on.

No, it was not Bob's ring tone. It was her friend Mary Browning in Austin.

"My God, Kathy! Are you guys okay?"

"I don't know. I don't know!"

"I just saw on the news it was your school. What is going on?"

"I don't know, I just saw it too."

"They're hitting a school in Austin. Not my son's but I'm going to get him out now," she cried, "They're hitting every school in the country!"

"Mary, I can't talk, I'm going to get Wendy and Bob."

She clicked the phone off and ran out the door. She realized that she still had Shelly in her arms, who was kicking and sobbing.

She turned to her neighbor's home. The Andersons? She didn't know them well. They were an older couple, their kids were off to college and the mother Elizabeth apparently stayed at home, that was about all she knew of them. A car was in the driveway. She ran to the house, rang the doorbell, waited a few seconds, then abandoned social convention and tried the doorknob and burst in.

"Kathy? What in God's name?"

Elizabeth stood at the top of stairs, hair disheveled, wearing yoga pants and a tee shirt, and was obviously confused. She most likely was enjoying the luxury of a nap while the world was going insane.

"Have you been watching the news?"

"No," and there was a slight edge of annoyance to her voice, "I was sleeping."

She descended the flight of stairs and was startled as Kathy stepped forward to try and hand off Shelly who was now worked up to a fever pitch of crying.

"Take Shelly. Please, I've got to go. I've got to get to the school!"

She literally shoved Shelly into Elizabeth's arms so fiercely that the older woman actually did clutch the child.

"Kathy, what is going on? Calm down."

"I can't calm down! Watch Shelly, please, and turn on the news."

She turned and ran out the door, leaving it open, jumping into the SUV. She fumbled with her pockets, then cursed foully. The keys. She ran back into the house, leaving her front door open and grabbed her purse, opening it. The keys were within, and also the Ruger that was identical to Bob's. She pushed the weapon into her pocket and as she did so she heard Shelly screaming nearby. Kathy turned to see Elizabeth entering the doorway, eyes going wide at the sight of Kathy pocketing the small weapon.

"Merciful heavens, Kathy, are you going insane?" and Kathy could see the woman was actually afraid and even protectively clutching Shelly tight against her shoulder.

"The world is insane…" she cried, pointing at the blaring television. She shouldered her way past Elizabeth and jumped into the car. Seconds later she was tearing down the driveway and was nearly T-boned by Denise Kilgore, another mother, whose only child was in first grade at McAuliffe Elementary school several blocks away from Chamberlain. All across the neighborhood, dozens of parents were getting into cars, tearing down driveways and office parking lots, and flooring it to McAuliffe Elementary, Perry High School, Chamberlain Middle School... not just in Portland but also to Oak Grove School in Vassalboro, Maine, to Tecumseh High in Lafayette Indiana, to Jackson elementary in Salem, Oregon... to thousands of schools across the country. The panic was on, just as the caliph had prophesied to his followers.

A news report from a school in Toledo, Ohio, came on the abandoned television, which reported a lockdown and shooting with one person dead so far. A possible attack, another similar report, came out of Savannah, Georgia. Both were actually panic-stricken parents, pulling up in front of their child's school and leaping out of their vehicles. Those two unfortunate people were both openly carrying guns and ignoring the shouted warning of panicky police officers who were racing to every school around the country, believing that they were arriving only seconds ahead of, or just behind, a potential attack. Both parents were shot dead in a fusillade of fire. It would take hours to sort out that they were not terrorists, only frightened parents, but their deaths added to the tally of schools reported as being under attack.

*Inside Joshua Chamberlain Middle School*

The door to Bob's classroom burst open and the terrorist, the barrel of his assault weapon poised low from the hip, stepped halfway into the room with a calm arrogance. He fired a shot to kill a child, the one already wounded in the arm and huddled in the corner of the room.

Bob leveled his palm-sized Ruger at him and fired from less than three feet away. Shaking, he missed. Missed completely.

His startled enemy actually stepped back. This was not supposed to be happening. The infidels were cowards, sheep. How could this be? He started to swing the muzzle of his rifle toward the side of the door, to fire through the flimsy plaster walls. Bob stepped forward, this time nearly pressing the muzzle of the Ruger into his opponent's face and squeezed the trigger. The shot caught the man in the jaw, shattering it in a spray of blood and teeth.

With a strangled cry, the attacker fell back into the hallway cursing, and a rapid spray of gunfire invaded the classroom. Every remaining window in the classroom shattered. Children huddled in the corner, out of the way of the barrage. Bob could actually see shell casings ejecting out in the hallway but the murderer whom he was certain he had hit was not visible.

"Come on you pig, you son of a bitch. Come on in!" Bob taunted.

No response, only labored breathing, choking and spitting, then the sound of a magazine dropping.

It registered in his mind but he did not have the instinct to react swiftly. Something told him that if he reacted instantly he would catch his enemy reloading, reeling from the shock of being hit, and finish him. But he did not have the training, to instantly press his attack, and he remained frozen in place for several crucial seconds, pistol raised, as if expecting his enemy to foolishly step into his line of fire yet again.

His opponent was still out in the hallway, heavy, raspy breathing, gasping for air, gagging as if choking, and in that crucial moment hesitating as well in disbelief that he had actually been wounded by a damned infidel. He slammed in a loaded magazine and chambered a round, the sound of it loud and clear to Bob over the wailing of the

60

fire alarm, the cries of the children, and the hissing of the sprinklers.

"Come on, you pig eater!" Bob screamed, trying to provoke him.

There was a grunted response, and a shout from down the hallway, sounding like a command from one of the other killers. Several seconds of silence followed. Bob waited tensely. Surely they had grenades of some kind and Bob was waiting for one to bounce into the room. He caught a glimpse out the window, hoping to see a reflection of who was in the hallway, but all of the windows had been blown out. He heard shooting outside, the sound of sirens now, and what must be a helicopter. Maybe that was help at last, a SWAT team or something?

Wendy? He couldn't see her.

Don't lose focus. Your death is on the other side of that open doorway. He actually had a reflective thought, amazed with how many thoughts struck him, that he knew what they meant about one's life flashing before them in their final seconds. That realization was a warning. He fell to the floor and as he did so, the wall space where he had been standing a second earlier was stitched by half a dozen bullets, plasterboard exploding across the room. He caught Patty's gaze, her surviving children clustered in the corner of the room around her. He motioned for them to stay down on the floor. They were all pinned, their unseen killer obviously injured, recoiling, and deciding on his next course of action.

Down low on the floor Bob waited, pistol aimed to shoot upward if the murderer made a dash through the doorway. There was no gunfire for more than half a minute, and then a new eruption of staccato bursts. But not aimed toward the room he was in. He heard the doorway to the faculty lounge being shot open, a few shots from within that small room, a pause, then more shots, this time apparently from the classroom across the hall next to the faculty lounge.

The bastard was pushing on with his killing, not coming back for him. Bastard! He had faced someone armed but now retreated to kill in other rooms.

"Come on you pig eater. Come on!" he screamed, trying to lure him away from his mission.

Then there was a sudden change to the sound. A shotgun? Half a dozen explosive shots rang out, children screaming, trapped in the corners of the room across the hall, and dying.

God, what do I do? he silently prayed. Hold here, at least I've got this room secure, or try and get the bastard and finish him? If he gets me these kids die. What do I do? he begged God as the sound of weapons shifted yet again. They were pistol shots and someone, he recognized the voice of Olivia Wilson, a mild bespectacled reading teacher, begged for mercy for her kids. Her cries were suddenly cut off.

God, do I hold here or try and stop him?

The answer finally came from within: get these kids out, then try and take the killer on again.

"Get the kids out now," he hissed to Patty, who finally nodded acknowledgement as he pointed to the shattered windows. Cop cars, half a dozen, were racing down the approach road to the school. He could see one of the vehicles being hit by fire, but at least that meant one of the murderer's attention was diverted.

"Patty, get the kids out now! I can't go after him until you're out of this room. I'll hold the door here while you get them out!"

# CHAPTER FIVE

As they had so adroitly planned, so clearly understanding their enemy far better than the enemy understood themselves, the highways were now flooding with traffic. There were over seventy million children, attending nearly one hundred thousand public schools in America. Millions more were in private, church, and parochial schools. The targets had been carefully chosen: to hit outside of major cities and in geographical locations so that no part of the country felt safe. All of the targets were very close to interstate highways, the route that so many parents would flock to within minutes to speed to the schools their children were in, whether that school was under attack or not.

The fear of school shootings had been a running nightmare in the heart of every parent since Columbine. Endless rounds of arguments and debates swirled around the scenario. It was those lone, sick killers in American schools across the previous two decades that had inspired the caliph with his plan. Nearly all had been psychotic American males from teens to early twenties. All were loners. Nearly all had fantasized online and obsessively spent hundreds of hours with the endless outpouring of America's entertainment media of shooter games and mass murder movies. Nearly all had played out a sick perverted fantasy in their final moments as they had became killers, usually vengeance for some slight from a girl, from a bully, or from the system. The killings were a power trip during their final moments that all would cower as they stalked the halls. And nearly all had ultimately proven themselves cowards in the caliph's eyes, either fleeing when the police arrived, or killing themselves like Hitler in his bunker.

And so the pattern of response in American schools had evolved: a plethora of "this campus is a gun-free zone." Drills and more drills, usually just with teachers, of course; no one wanted to frighten the children, even though they saw the news every night and chatted about it on Facebook. Lock the door, lie down, wait for rescue. A few will die, maybe even a few dozen, but the vast majority will be saved by lying down and waiting for others to come to the rescue.

The brilliance of the caliph's plan was understanding the pattern of the infidels' reaction, how they would respond collectively to a threat to their precious children. They usually had just one or two offspring, not six or eight with a willingness to see their progeny sacrificed to Allah's will. No, for them each child was precious, doted upon, and coddled. The parents across the entire nation would react, the nation falling into mass panic. Unlike the fool bin Laden's attack on 9/11, every American would feel personally threatened, not just those living in New York and Washington. Every American in those first moments would fear that their precious child was about to become a target as well. Though only a few out of nearly one hundred thousand schools were now threatened, millions of parents would rush out of their homes and their offices and flood onto the interstates.

The frenzy would build. The planners had calculated it well and had laughed over it. Thus it now unfolded and the time to launch Sword Two had come.

There was no need to send the final message, all who were trained knew the exact moment, but in his arrogant delight he ordered the message to be sent anyhow: "*Sword Two.*" After sending the message, the transmitting phone was left active in the corner of a captured Christian church near Raqqa, the messenger laughing as he drove off.

Sword Two had already begun in some places such as Austin, Syracuse, and near Portland Maine, ahead of schedule. Attack teams began to pull out of hotel parking lots which, in less than a minute, put them on the American interstates, highways built as copies of the German autobahns, ironically ordered as a defense measure in the event of a nuclear attack by the Soviet Union.

Sword Two was made up of teams of two to three jihadist martyrs. There was a driver, armed with a 9mm pistol for a final defense, and one or two gunmen armed with AK-47s, each with thirty or more clips of jacketed rounds. Simply get on the highway, swing alongside cars, preferably those with a number of passengers, and shoot the driver. Tractor trailers were sweet targets: drive up, send several shots through the door, then speed on, hoping the truck jackknifes. Even better if it is carrying petrol or some hazardous material.

The team that roared onto Interstate 40 near Knoxville headed east for the connection to Interstate 81 and hit their jackpot in the first two minutes. A tractor trailer hauling petrol swerved out of control, the holy warrior laughing that he had hit the driver in the head with his first shot. All of the mayhem that ensued was created by a single 7.62 round fired from a Kalashnikov. That opening move proved how simple the plan was, how effective it was, and it created joyful anticipation of all that they could accomplish in the next few hours.

The truck crashed through the flimsy highway barrier into the westbound lanes, rolling over, gasoline spilling out, bursting into flames and seconds later exploding. Two more trucks were taken out by the Knoxville attack team in less than a minute, one on each side of the highway, sealing the road off in both directions.

Two hundred miles further east, on I-40, a Sword Two unit was now working in cooperation with the Sword One unit that had stormed an elementary school several miles to the west of Hickory. From the highway they could see that the school was burning and traffic was backed up on the exit ramp. The American parents were in complete panic; apparently an accident occurred at the top of the ramp blocking the exit. Vehicles were swinging on to the grassy berm to get around the bottleneck, but since it had rained heavily the night before, many were bogging down, wheels spinning.

The team of three actually broke their trained procedure for the moment, so rich was their target now. Coming to a stop, one of the killers shot the driver of the car behind them and triggered a chain reaction accident involving several dozen cars.

The jihadists then exited their vehicle and stood along the side of the road, calling on their god, laughing as they turned the traffic jam at the exit ramp into target practice, one ordering the other to take aimed single shots and not waste ammunition on such easy targets. Several dozen frantic parents were slaughtered in little more than a minute. It was almost too easy, they thought, as they got back into their car and pressed on westward.

Nearly all of the other teams stuck to their training in those first minutes. On Interstate 287, the outer ring of New York City, thirty cars were taken off the road in the first five minutes. At a jammed exit ramp near the school under attack in Bakersfield, California, nearly as many parents were now dead as students in the school.

In reality, the casualty rate in the schools was just now beginning to soar as captive children were herded into the gym, to drag out the agony of what the response team thought would be negotiations. All negotiations were a sham of course; a knife could kill quietly, even gruesomely, while those surrounding the building outside heard nothing from the locker rooms where the slaughter was taking place, and thought they were talking their opponents into laying down their weapons.

Lancaster, Pennsylvania, Wheeling, West Virginia, Birmingham, Alabama, Little Rock, Arkansas, Crete, Nebraska, Salt Lake City, Utah, Phoenix, Arizona, and along remote stretches of highway such as south of Valdosta, Georgia, and northward along I-77 into West Virginia, the thirty-plus teams of Sword Two were unleashing death. The roads were packed with parents bent on reaching their children, most not even seeing death racing up behind them or about to pass in the opposite direction.

Only one team of Sword Two had been completely stopped in those first minutes due to a random encounter with a county sheriff in an unmarked car near Kingston, New York. It was one of those "one in a million" moments, but all plans, even the best laid ones, are prone to a random factor. The officer had served four tours of duty in Iraq and Afghanistan with a military police unit. He, like nearly every police officer in America, was racing to secure a community school in the minutes after Sword One was unleashed. As he approached the entry ramp over the interstate, which at this location was part of the New York Turnpike, he saw the attack vehicle with its two gunmen who were heading to the Turnpike to start their attack.

A flash of recognition.

What drew his attention were the windows of the vehicle. All of them were down and the day was chilly. He looked closer. Could the man in the passenger seat actually be that particularly troublesome bastard from the prison near Baghdad, one who had taunted him back in 2009, when the administration decided to release thousands of such prisoners, that they would meet again, in America? There was a brief instant of eye contact and the way the man reacted caught him now as well. Even innocent folks would do a bit of a double take if they suddenly realized that a police officer was staring at them. But guilty of something? They would either try to brazen it out by staring back with an "I ain't done nothing wrong so why in hell are you looking at me," look or a quick furtive turning away of the eyes, acting as if they had not seen him, but then catching occasional sidelong glances to see if he was still studying them.

This one started the nervous sidelong glances, then turned to say something to the driver of the car, looking back over his shoulder as their car sped down the entry ramp. They were wearing black and it looked as if there were shoulder straps for vests, the type of vests used for combat gear.

Procedure as a county sheriff was to call the Turnpike police, but to hell with procedure on this day! He swung his vehicle about and raced onto the Turnpike in pursuit. They were already speeding up. Only months earlier, sitting up at two in the morning, he had watched the video released by ISIS showing them blowing cars off a major highway while music in praise of their god played. It was expert video, filmed with Go-Pro cameras, with laughter and taunts as background noise as they machine-gunned carloads of refugees.

And now the slaughter was about to happen here. It was confirmed by puffs of smoke, followed by a car that they were passing swerving off the highway, fragments of broken glass spilling across the road. He radioed in the report, what he was going to do, and, without throwing on his lights he accelerated quickly, ramming the back of the attacker's car.

He eased back on the gas for several seconds; his car was loaded with a lot more horsepower than the jihadists', and then swung to their left. The gunman leaned out the open window to shoot him, but the former MP knew his game, ducking low as a couple of shots shattered his windshield. He floored the gas pedal, advanced to near parallel with the killers, cut hard across, and rammed the side of their car. The two vehicles spun out of control. The three jihadists and the sheriff were dead a few seconds later.

It was the only complete failure for ISIS in the opening minutes of Sword Two.

*Near Portland, Maine*

The incessant ringing of her cell phone finally jarred Kathy Petersen out of her hysteria. She had been leaning on the horn of her car for several minutes, cursing the driver in front of her for blocking the entry ramp to the interstate. The overpass to the entry ramp was packed with stalled traffic. The phone call was again from her friend Mary Browning; she ignored it, looking up to realize that the driver she had been swearing at was out of his car, walking back to her.

Instinctively she reached for the pistol tucked into her jeans pocket. Was he one of them?

She held the pistol up and the man slowed, raising his hands, actually appearing to smile nervously as he stepped backward several feet then slowly motioned for her to roll her window down.

"Hey look lady, don't blame me, the road ahead is blocked. Can you back up so I can get out of this jam?"

He again motioned for her to lower her pistol, which

she did, then pointed forward, repeating his appeal.

He was right, cars were backed up across the entire approach to the interstate. A state police car, just out of sight until now, blocked the road, lights flashing.

"I have to get to my daughter and husband's school!" she cried.

"Which one?"

"Chamberlain Middle."

"That's where I'm heading too. Can you back up?"

She got out and looked to the vehicle behind her, the driver staring at her and shouting for her to move. Kathy went to try and talk to her but the woman refused to roll her window down, screaming at her to move it.

It was gridlock. And then she heard it, sirens approaching fast from the southbound side. They rocketed under the overpass bridge that she was standing on, one of them skidding to a stop while the other pressed on, banking his car across two lanes to block traffic.

Someone pointed to a plume of smoke that suddenly ignited a mile or so away, screaming that it was the school on fire. She knew the school was more to the right, on the south side of the highway, not the north side, but the hysteria took hold. Whatever was burning was on the highway.

Sirens again. The state trooper who had stopped down on the highway was out of his vehicle, carrying a rifle, bracing it across the hood of his car. Southbound, cars were moving fast, driven as if every driver were drunk. Flashing blue lights became visible and a dark blue sedan appeared, swerving across two lanes, moving to pass a green SUV. A crackle of gunshots sounded and the side window of the SUV shattered, the car swerving into a sideways skid, the blue sedan racing past it at over ninety miles an hour. The cop down on the highway opened fire, tracking the sedan, but his half dozen shots apparently had no effect. There was only gunfire flashing from the sedan's rear passenger window in reply.

Those around Kathy ran to the other side of the overpass, shouting that the sedan was getting away, screaming impotent curses at it while down on the interstate the trooper who had stopped was back into his car, driving through a cut across into the southbound side, joining in the procession of a dozen police cars still in pursuit.

The shot-up SUV was on its side, crashed into the grassy berm. No one was stopping to help, if help was possible.

"You still for Chamberlain Middle, lady?"

She looked back at the middle aged man, dressed in typical "Mainer business": a blue blazer and shirt with no tie, chinos, and boat shoes.

"Yes."

"My son is a student there. Seventh grade. Let's see if we can get around this on back roads."

She got back into her car and tried to back up but there was less than a foot to spare. She backed up as far as she could until bumpers hit. It gave the man in front of her just enough room to start squeezing his small Fiat back and forth before breaking free of the gridlock, turning about to head in the opposite direction. He actually drove with two wheels up on the walkway as he squeezed between two stalled SUVs similar to hers.

She sat in her car, not sure whether to wish him good luck or curse him for the way he was taking off. But he stopped, rolled down his window, and motioned for her to get in.

Without a second thought she abandoned her car, leaving the keys in the ignition so someone could move it if the road was ever cleared. She ran to the passenger side of her benefactor's car and squeezed in.

"Never thought I'd like this car, wife insisted we buy it to save on gas," he offered as she buckled herself into the narrow seat.

"If it gets us through this, I'll buy one."

"I'm Craig Sullivan, my boy John is at Chamberlain."

"Kathy Petersen, my daughter Wendy is in seventh grade, my husband Bob teaches there. We've got to get there now."

"I know Bob, my son thinks the world of him."

There was a moment of silence as he squeezed around a stalled dump truck.

"Could you switch on my pad so we can check the reporting from the school?"

She had forgotten to bring hers as she had rushed out the door and was glad to have the link. She picked up his pad from the floor, switched it on, and found the website of a local news station.

"To repeat the latest news: The governor of Maine has just announced that all schools in the state are in lockdown mode. He has appealed to parents to not approach any school to try and retrieve their children at this time. I am asked to repeat that. Parents are not to try and go to any school within the state. All schools are in lockdown. No one in, no one out. The governor stated that law enforcement have been scrambled to every school, public and private, throughout the state and the children within are secured and safe. No child is to be released until it is felt that the situation is firmly under control.

"We have several reports now, one from Sanford, Maine, others from outside the state, of parents being mistaken for terrorists and shot. The situation, needless to say, is tense. If you are going to your child's school, please stop and go home. Your presence can do nothing to help protect your child and might actually hinder our law enforcement and emergency personnel."

She lowered the volume and looked in inquiry over at Craig.

"Screw that," he snapped. "Chamberlain is in the middle of this and under attack. I told my son that if the crap ever hit the fan, he was to get out of the school and to hell with what any teacher or administrator said."

He looked at her, realizing as he spoke that her husband was one of said teachers and that his comment might provoke an angry retort.

She nodded her head.

"Agreed. We go to the school," and she turned the volume up to monitor the news while Craig pressed in the direction of the school.

The rapidly escalating national panic was fueled even more when one over-excited, self-aggrandizing reporter, who had nearly created a debacle in New Orleans during Katrina when he hysterically reported a total descent into anarchy in the emergency shelter established in the "Superdome," was now crying that he believed that the attacks were spreading to dozens of schools and that thousands of children were being slaughtered across the nation.

His pronouncement quickly morphed into a report of fact as it leapt to the social internet sites, causing millions more to give way to their fears and ignore the logical warnings of state governors.

There was a time when a public official might actually have been trusted, such as the voice of Franklin Delano Roosevelt the day after December 7th, and again Rudy Guiliani in the hours after the World Trade Center had been hit. But whom was actually trusted now?

Who was trusted when, every day yet a new scandal was revealed? Even before the killing started on this day, public trust in public officials was at its lowest in the history of the Republic.

Easy enough for a governor to say stay at home, was the first response of millions. His kids are in private school with 24/7 armed security around them. Members of Congress on up to the President? Their kids were in the most expensive Quaker school in the country in an upscale neighborhood of D.C. Few commented how ironic it was, that a religion devoted to complete non-violence, even in the face of this kind of attack, was the most heavily armed and secured school campus in the country, with security posted there round the clock, even in the middle of the night. Any attacker would face a firestorm of steel, complete with helicopter support, within seconds.

Who are they to tell us to stay home when our children are dying and theirs are protected?

And so the roads continued to fill up.

To add to the irony of it all, the news feed switched to Washington D.C., with a long-distance shot of a helicopter landing on the front lawn of that upscale school in Washington, a flurry of movement around it, heavily armed security forming a perimeter, a reporter announcing that the children of the President were thankfully safe and being airlifted "to an undisclosed location."

Kathy watched the brief clip, incredulous at the insensitivity of it all. Never, ever would she wish harm upon that man's innocent children. But it was an aloof display of the arrogance of power, as if she was to feel relief that at least his children were well protected, while at this very moment, her daughter could be wounded or dead, her husband, wounded or dead. Neither had a swarm of

74

Secret Service agents, marine-piloted helicopters and, undoubtedly at this moment, attack helicopters and fighters, circling over Chamberlain Middle School.

She was jolted out of her resentful thoughts as Craig slammed on the brakes and turned the wheel. They were driving through a residential neighborhood, flanking the interstate, where traffic was at a complete standstill. The smoke plume they had seen in the distance was now visible, a multi-vehicle pileup on the roadway.

Directly in front of them a pickup truck had run a stop sign, not even slowing, skidded to make the turn, fishtailing, and slammed into a car headed the other way. Craig dodged the wreck, adroitly hitting the gas to regain control, and narrowly missed a man running down the middle of the street in the direction of the school. Then he sped up again.

She looked back at the pad.

"Back to our network headquarters in New York..."

There was a pause for what seemed like an eternity. The network had already created a logo, "America Under Attack."

The logo snapped off, replaced by the familiar, comforting anchor for the network's mid-afternoon programming. It was obvious, though, that he was struggling for the composure to convey calm, particularly after the hysterical report of one of their reporters minutes earlier claimed that attacks against schools were spreading across the nation.

He identified himself then pressed straight in:

"We have received reports from affiliates across the nation that numerous schools are under some form of attack. However, I can state clearly that only five of these have been confirmed and identified as ongoing attacks, contrary to some reports from this network."

It was obvious he was furious over the hysterical report of minutes earlier claiming mass attacks across the country.

"The names of the schools which we have confirmed are under attack are listed at the bottom of your screen. Even if your child is in one of those schools, government officials implore you not to go there until the situation is under control. If your child's school is not on this list, please remain at home and off the highways.

Kathy felt hesitation and looked over at Craig. His jaw line set as he swerved around a three-car accident at the next intersection.

"We're going," he confirmed, and she nodded, saying nothing.

"A new dimension to this day is now unfolding. Reports are starting to come in that while police attention across the nation has been focused on securing our schools, attacks have spread to our interstate highway system. So far over two dozen affiliates are reporting drive-by shootings on interstate highways. There is no discernible pattern to the locations of these attacks. Many of these attacks are taking place hundreds of miles away from any of the schools that we know are under siege.

"The nature of the highway attacks is identical to reports we broadcasted back in the spring when the terrorist army of ISIS moved into northern Iraq."

As he spoke a box taking up half of the screen flashed on, time stamped from early June and filmed from the interior of a car, of barrels of AK-47s stuck out of side windows and Middle Eastern music playing. The murderers were shouting and laughing as they drove up alongside an orange car, and then a hail of gunfire poured into it. The car swerved off the road, accompanied by laughter and shouts of glee and cries of "Allahu akbar!" as the orange car, riddled with bullet holes, crashed.

"We have footage of such attacks from our affiliate in Austin, Texas, and from Knoxville, Tennessee, taken by news helicopters."

The box showing the first attack was replaced by two smaller ones, video shot from helicopters, showing a massive conflagration on Interstate 40 filmed just east of Knoxville, Tennessee, engulfing both sides of the highway, dozens of cars piled up. The second small-screen footage was of a vehicle pursued by four or five police cars, passing a white sedan, gunfire striking the sedan which then swerved and slammed into the pillar of an overpass.

The screen returned to full size.

"Even as I am speaking to you, my producer is telling me that more footage is coming in from Daytona, Florida, and Dover, Delaware, of similar attacks."

He paused and it was obvious he was not acting for dramatic effect. His voice was trembling, near to breaking.

"In light of what we are now seeing, I must personally say that America is facing a coordinated attack by a foreign enemy. There is no hard evidence yet, but I will lay my career on the line with this, that we are facing the long-anticipated and publicly announced attack that ISIS has been threatening us with for months. It is either ISIS or a radical group associated with them. This horrific attack bears the markings of mass murderers without regard for any concept of civilized behavior.

"I therefore appeal to all of you to do two things. First, pray to God that this scourge shall speedily pass away."

That shocked Kathy. His words were both Lincolnesque but also unheard of in this current age. A reporter asking his listeners to appeal to God? An ironic thought that even now, within minutes, the network would probably be flooded with text messages and phone calls demanding that the reporter be fired for "jamming" his religious views down the throats of his audience and that he make an on-air apology for it.

"And second, I appeal to you that if you are on the road, trying to reach your children in schools, please, pull over, stop, and take a deep breath."

He paused, obviously welling up.

"I cannot leave here to try to reach my kids, though every fiber of my being as a father is screaming at me to do so."

He paused, lowering his head for a moment. In television, even a few seconds of silence felt like an eternity and it was a good ten seconds before he regained his composure to face the camera again.

"We need to take a break..." was all he could now muster.

Kathy looked at Craig, for a moment filled with doubt about what they were doing.

"We aren't going any further," he announced. She wondered if he was indeed abandoning their quest and was ready to turn about. If so, she would tell him to stop, get out and run the rest of the way. Their school, her daughter's school, her husband's school, was confirmed as being under attack. It was not a rumor, it was not a fear, it was confirmed and she had to be there.

Craig skidded to a stop and she looked up again. It was not that he was giving up. They were still a quarter mile out from Chamberlain Middle, but the road ahead was jammed bumper-to-bumper, red taillights glowing, frantic parents getting out of their cars, abandoning them in the traffic jam, deciding to run toward the chaos. Ambulances and police cars were driving across lawns and walkways, sirens wailing. It was a cacophony of madness.

She got out of the car, a bit startled when Craig actually grabbed her shoulder.

"Come on!" he cried, and she started to run with him. She felt as if her heart were about to burst, for in the distance she could hear the repetitive bursts of gunfire.

Her husband, her daughter were in the deepest circle of hell.

*Inside Joshua Chamberlain Middle School*

The gunfire ceased in the room across the hall; Bob could hear muffled child-voiced moans and cries, heartbreaking, so many calls for "mommy" as they died. Mommy, who, when they were at the arrogant age of twelve and thirteen, was a source of embarrassment and eye rolling when an attempt was made to kiss and hug them in public, but in a moment of terror, of pain, of dying? It was a cry to a mother for comfort, to hold them and to ease the pain as they died, and it steeled Bob for what he had to do. He was so shocked by the anguish of it all that he first had to wipe tears from his eyes, silently cursing himself for his moment of frozen inaction and fear.

How could any man, any human being inflict such suffering upon children? He could hear the triumphal calls to their Allah echoing down the hallway and it filled him with rage and now the motivation to move aggressively and fight back. All the years of political correctness, all the appeals from the nation's leaders to extend a hand of friendship to all... If really true, where was the righteous anger now? In the same way Christians by the tens of thousands rose up in anger against the evils of the Westboro Church that harassed the families of dead soldiers returning home in caskets from the Middle East, and taunted gays and anyone who was different?

He had enough of an interest in history to recall, even

in these few seconds, Winston Churchill's sarcastic response and warnings against the appeasement of his nation's leader in 1938 and the terrible price it would eventually cost Great Britain and the free world.

And that price had now come due again, literally in the corridors of his school, his daughter's school, and he was at the very tip of the spear of that price. And now he prayed that in the next few seconds he could do something, anything, to slow them down, to buy time and, if need be, to die, to die well doing what was right.

He checked on Patty, who was guiding her charges up and out of the shattered window, encouraging each to run the moment they hit the ground. To his horror, he saw two of them drop, caught in the gunfire raging outside the building, but the others were making it through. It did not take a trained expert to know that a moving target was infinitely harder to hit than one cowering in a corner or lying prone on the floor. If some of them were getting through, it was better than waiting here for certain death.

Patty's gaze caught his eye as she helped the last child up to the window before climbing out herself. She was crying, staring straight at him.

"God be with you, Bob," she mouthed the words, nearly silent, then turned to drop out the window behind the last of her children.

There were six more classrooms down the long hall beyond the one he was holed up in, plus the room across the hallway where the murderer was finishing off the last of his victims. He prayed that the teachers in those rooms had followed Patty's lead, but knew they had not. One was Margaret Redding's classroom. Last he had seen her, she was cowering in the faculty lounge, her teaching assistant left in charge of the classroom. That poor, harried elderly woman was afraid of her own shadow and would follow every order by Margaret, which would include ordering the children to lie down as sheep and await slaughter.

He saw no other children sprinting across the playground. There was no view to the other side of the building but he had to assume that far too many classrooms still had victims waiting for their executioner, who would call out to his alleged god as he put a 9mm bullet into the head of each child before moving on to the next room. He could hear the sirens outside, the thumping of at least one helicopter which he hoped would bring succor. He did not know that it was a news helicopter filming and transmitting the insanity rather than a SWAT team, which, in reality, was still forming up in downtown Portland and not yet in the air.

The shooting and screams in the room across the hallway stopped. The fire alarm was still wailing its incessant numbing shriek, sprinklers continuing to douse the corridor. He was down flat on the floor at the doorway, pistol raised, aimed at the open doorway across the hall. He kept going over in his head the training he had received for the concealed permit: breathe in, half exhale, aim and squeeze... breathe in, half exhale. But it did not still the hyperventilation of fear and nervousness. Three bullets, I've got three bullets. He has hundreds. Breathe, half exhale. Hail Mary, full of grace...

He started to pray, though it had been years since he last attended mass, on the day he and Kathy married.

A tall, dark shadow appeared in the doorway across the hall.

Now!

He squeezed off two rounds, aimed straight at the chest, the center of the body. The shadow staggered backwards for a moment but then just came forward toward the doorway where Bob was waiting. A flash moment of terror. What in hell was this, the "Terminator," indestructible? The murderer's weapon lowered, aimed straight at him. He saw the muzzle flash, a terrible shock struck him in the back. His lower body went numb.

Armor, he has body armor! Bob was in that instant inwardly amazed that he could recognize such a thing as he looked up, saw his opponent drawing closer, weapon at the shoulder, aiming down to deliver a killing shot to his head before moving on to murder more children.

Bob pointed his pistol straight up and squeezed off the last round, his bullet striking his foe just below the left eye, killing him instantly, so that the jihadist staggered backwards and collapsed into the room where he had been so gleefully slaughtering the defenseless but seconds earlier.

Bob laid in shock for long seconds, empty pistol aimed at the recumbent body across the school corridor, the legs of his enemy twitching spasmodically for several seconds before going still. He kept the pistol aimed at him, not yet registering that the slide of his pistol was fully back, indicating his weapon was empty. When he did realize it, there was a brief thought to look about on the floor for the single unfired cartridge he had ejected earlier. The floor around him was slick with blood. It was not registering yet that it was his own blood commingled with the blood of his enemy from his first shot to the jaw.

There was silence in the building except for the wailing cry of the fire alarm. Was there any way to turn that damn thing off? he wondered. Sprinklers in the hallway were still spraying out a mist of water, diluting the rivulets of blood seeping out of the scores of children, the principal, and the two teachers lying dead in the corridor.

More firing, thundering loud from down by the administrative area. He dared to peek out from the cover of the doorway. No jihadist was in sight but there was someone firing from that area, while from outside the building he heard sirens and what sounded like more gunfire.

A shadow, a dark face covered with a ski mask, appeared at the end of the hallway, shouting something that he assumed was Arabic. A query, an order? Another call. A sparkle-like effect appeared on the wall above him. Bullets fired from outside were impacting above the killer. The face disappeared and a couple of seconds later there was a sustained burst of automatic fire in reply.

Bob continued to look down the corridor. Was that the pathetic looking body of Mr. Carl in the middle of the hallway, blank eyes staring at him with warning, reproach, or orders to keep going, to keep fighting back?

He had seen three killers storming his building. Three against five hundred and thirty children and thirty-seven adults. He had without doubt dropped one of the killers, but that meant that two remained.

Chechnya. This was not some random act of madness. This was a well-planned attack by jihadists. Their mission was to kill as many defenseless innocents as possible before they themselves were taken to paradise. They were remorseless murderers. There would be no negotiating, for negotiating simply bought time to inflict more killing. He recalled a discussion on a news channel, a commentator who was bitterly denounced by various "friendship with Islam" organizations afterwards quoting their Koran, that ultimately negotiations with infidels were simply a ploy until true believers gained control and then the infidels were to submit or die. All bargaining was a sham, for each bargain would be a step backwards. The only way he could bargain now was to somehow get a weapon and continue to fight back.

Two killers still at large in his school and he had an empty gun. A complete sense of impotence overwhelmed him for a moment. At least his daughter's class had gotten out. Wendy? He did not even know if she had made it through the kill zone or not and the thought of that filled him with rage.

Bastards. Damn cowardly bastards. Target us, the adults in the Trade Center and the Pentagon. But this was a step beneath the gutter of all of humanity. They had brought their hell to Chamberlain Middle School near Portland, Maine.

Chamberlain. Joshua Lawrence Chamberlain. How few knew that their school was actually named after a hero of the Civil War, a holder of the Medal of Honor for his gallantry and leadership at Gettysburg. There was supposed to be a ritual each year to honor his memory but few paid attention when it was held and many grumbled that it took time out from the pressing need to prepare the students for the next battery of mandatory testing.

Taking time to honor some dead guy of a hundred and fifty years ago? There were other things far more important.

He had a memory of reading about Chamberlain, how when his regiment was out of ammunition, facing five times their number charging up the hill that they were ordered to hold at all costs, he had come to what was the only logical conclusion. He had ordered his men to fix bayonets and charge.

The terrifying reality that the shot put into his back had paralyzed him was beginning to sink in. Charging was out. But less than twenty feet away there was at least one gun and plenty of ammunition.

He could still block this corridor against the other murderers for a few more precious minutes until help arrived.

He started to drag his body across the water-and-blood-soaked hallway. And then the pain hit, agonizing, terrifying. He could see Mr. Carl, his sightless eyes staring at him. In spite of the shrieking of the fire alarm, the spray of water cascading down, he could hear the gunfire, the sound of hot shell casings ejecting onto the checkerboard flooring by the foyer, and more distant firing coming from the other wing of the school. With his gaze fixed down the corridor, he continued to crawl, foot by agonizing foot, toward the man he had just killed, who still held in his blood-stained hands the means to salvation, for at least a few more minutes.

A distant shadowed face appeared again at the end of the corridor, staring straight at him. To Bob, his eyes looked to be the eyes of Satan incarnate on earth, remorseless and cold as a serpent's... The killer aimed his weapon.

# CHAPTER SIX

As she ran, Kathy's phone beeped yet again. Still not Bob; it was a text message from Mary Browning: "Please talk, please!"

She ignored the appeal for the moment. There was a line of flashing blue lights ahead, a crowd shouting, arguing with two police officers who were announcing over and over that no one could approach the building. And then, as if to add emphasis to their argument, there was a sustained burst of firing from within the school, which was visible only a few hundred yards farther down the road. A woman close to one of the officers staggered, clutching her stomach, that officer going down as well, and the side window of a patrol car shattered.

That set off a panicked run of a hundred or more back toward Kathy. Swept up in the crowd, she was pushed backwards. She managed to break free of the stampede of frightened parents as the road reached an intersection. A patrol car had just pulled up to the intersection, the officer got out with a bullhorn raised, shouting that an emergency waiting area had been established just up the road, and aggressively motioned the crowd to turn and get out of the line of fire. Up a side street she saw a small crowd in front of a Catholic church where someone else was announcing on a megaphone that it was a gathering place for parents. Kathy, with Craig by her side, followed the crowd. An elderly police officer was outside urging parents to get into the church which was being set up as an official waiting area. A priest stood by the open door of the church's recreation hall.

"In here please, wait in here," the harried priest kept repeating over and over, the double doors braced wide open. From the main approach to the school there was a constant wail of sirens, ambulances coming in from half a dozen communities, driving over lawns and then jamming up, unable to get closer.

It was a sea of confusion and terror. Two helicopters were circling the school a couple of hundred yards away, both of them with logos of their respective news stations.

Pushed along by the crowd, she entered the jammed recreation hall. A television on one wall was broadcasting a local news report, the noise in the room was so loud no one could hear. Arguments were breaking out and people were shouting for everyone to shut up.

A talking head was on the screen, a local news anchor. Someone had thought to turn on closed captioning and she read the report:

"The Governor has just ordered that all of Interstate 95 has been shut down. Anyone attempting to get on the interstate will be stopped and arrested. If you are on the interstate now exit immediately. There are confirmed reports of a shooter or shooters in a dark blue sedan, a late model Ford or Chevy four-door now south of Falmouth, traveling southbound and shooting at vehicles on both sides of the road. There are reports of numerous injuries and fatalities. I repeat: the governor has ordered Interstate 95 from the New Hampshire border to Houlton, Maine, is closed to all but emergency traffic. If you are on the interstate, exit immediately."

Her phone beeped again, it was Mary, but this time she answered.

"My God, they are killing people on the highway now!" Mary cried.

"I know, I know," Kathy replied absently, her attention focused on the television.

"I'm trying to get to Arthur's school. Thank God it's not his school being hit, but I just know they'll go there next."

"Mary, get off the road. They're shutting the interstate here, I assume they will there. There are killers on the road in your area. Your boy is in a safe school, so go home, damn it!"

"How am I to know that? Trust that?" she cried.

"Mary, listen to me…"

The signal went dead.

*Interstate 35, north of Austin, Texas*

The cell phone networks across the entire United States were overloading, tens of millions of calls began to drop; the one to her friend Kathy in Maine was one of them. Mary tried to call again, but there was no signal. That sent an additional wave of fear through her. Were they somehow attacking or jamming communications as well?

The traffic was slowing to a crawl, bumper to bumper, more than a few cars swinging onto the shoulders and grass-covered berm. She could now see the exit that she wanted still a mile off, traffic was backed up around it. Undoubtedly nearly a thousand parents like her were heading to the same school to snatch their children out of harm's way.

Local news had already announced the order that the interstates across all of Texas were being shut down, that every school in the state had gone to full lockdown and no parent would be permitted anywhere near any school for the rest of the afternoon. But, like millions of other parents, she did not trust all that she heard. Regarding the interstate, what were they going to do, arrest a million people? Regarding her son's school, at least she and other parents would, if need be, form a human barrier and, this being Texas, it would be a heavily armed barrier, until such time as the authorities relented and let them take their children to safety.

She drifted at just twenty miles an hour beneath an overpass and as she cleared it she saw in her rear view mirror a police car come to a stop on the overpass, an officer leaping out of his vehicle.

A helicopter was visible in her rearview mirror as well, turning to circle the overpass that was now a hundred yards behind her. She turned her phone back on, went to her local news station's website and several seconds later she was looking at live video, transmitted from the circling helicopter, of a black sedan driving on the left shoulder a half mile or so behind her. She saw puffs of smoke and shattered glass flying from the vehicles the sedan was passing. The camera lens widened, a half mile or more farther back, to a place she had just passed several minutes ago: a tractor trailer was burning fiercely, blocking the road, and a half dozen police cars were trapped on the far side. The cops were out, trying to get drivers to move their cars off the road to clear a path for them to swing around the wreck and resume the chase.

The camera shifted to the overpass she had just cleared. The cop she had spotted was leaning over the railing, firing straight down at a vehicle racing along the left shoulder, scraping against the guard rail. His shots appeared to hit because steam suddenly blew out of the hood.

Traffic ahead of her came to a halt. She could see the woman driving beside her, holding up her phone, fixated on the screen, the same channel she was watching. Car doors were opening, drivers were abandoning their vehicles and running in panic.

Mary looked in her side mirror and saw the shot-up sedan approaching, slowing down...

A voice of caution within was screaming to her to get out, to run to the far side of the road and take cover as others were doing. But, mesmerized, she did not move, sinking into the mental trap of disbelief, that surely this could not be happening for real, to her.

The driver of the car in front of her, an elderly man, started to get out of his vehicle, moving slowly.

She had no place to go, her thoughts beginning to lock up. Pull onto the left shoulder and floor it? But I want the exit on the right! Duck down, they won't see me? Get out and run? Do something!

Instead she just sat in frozen silence, not understanding even herself, not remembering the question that so many asked in history classes when seeing old footage of the Nazis lining up victims, Al-Qaeda lining up victims, ISIS lining up victims. As to why, in that final moment, hardly anyone ever fought back? It was like the rabbit gazing into the eyes of the rattlesnake, whose eyes were death.

The mind starts to blank at the terrible reality of it all, that this was truly death approaching at last. Not peaceful death slipping in like a shadowy fog, while one was reconciled with one's final moments and surrounded by loved ones. It was death in its most brutal, ugly, dark face of man's inhumanity to man, unbelievable in its dreadful enormity. No matter what one might have wondered before this moment as to why those about to die so often knelt meekly, there was, when it came your turn to kneel, a strange detachment. Perhaps it was such disbelief that surely this was not happening and a miracle would occur, or just the mind shutting down entirely in the face of this final reality. One who did not believe in God would say it was a final chemical reaction within the brain, to still the struggling, while one who did believe in God might argue it was a gift, to blank out the horror of the final moment.

Steam was venting from the grill of the vehicle and out of the puncture holes blown into the hood. The sedan came to a stop on the shoulder two vehicles behind her. Doors popped open and three men, black clad, got out, weapons raised, one reaching back in to scoop up several black duffel bags. They paused for a few seconds looking about and then the eyes of the serpent gazed into hers looking back at them in the side view mirror of her car.

One ran the few feet to her car and leveled his rifle at her. She sat, just staring back, frozen. He shouted something, motioned with his rifle, shouted again.

"Get out, we won't hurt you. Get out!"

She didn't move.

He grabbed the door handle; it was locked.

With his free hand he pointed the rifle straight at her.

"Out now or I shoot!"

She finally did as ordered, and unlatched the door. He pulled it open, reached in and grabbed her roughly by the shoulder.

"It's yours," she gasped. "Please, it's yours! Just let me get out. The keys are still in it."

Her seat belt was holding her in.

"Get out. I won't shoot if you get out!"

She began to cry, fumbling with the release buckle, so terrified she was not even aware that in her fear she had just urinated, soaking the seat. He pulled her roughly out of the car.

"You bastard, let her go!"

This was met an instant later by the explosive roar of a gun going off behind her and she began to scream. One of the other two men approaching her car with his rifle shouldered had just put a round into the old man, who had come to a stop in front of her. He had drawn an old-style revolver to shoot her assailant, but the revolver flew from his grasp as he collapsed.

He had been part of a different world, of the mindset that a man protected a woman, and if the confrontation escalated to guns, you told the bastard to let the woman go or you were dead. It was the culture of a different world that even at that moment, you offered a final negotiation before someone died. But they were of a far different world and the old man was a fool. If he had moved silently he actually could have killed at least one of them before the other two riddled his body with bullets.

The two piled into the backseat of her BMW, tossing the duffel bags loaded with ammunition into the front passenger seat. One of the two was leaking blood from his right arm; he had been hit a few minutes back by the police that had been pursuing them.

The driver tossed his rifle onto the front passenger seat, then turned to look back. The cop up on the overpass was now firing toward them, but without effect. A news helicopter was overhead and he could see a camera man leaning out, pointing his camera straight down at him. The driver knew it was being broadcasted, locally perhaps, with luck even nationally. They had, of course, been monitoring the same channel on the pads that they carried.

He actually looked up and offered a friendly wave and then, knowing that it was being filmed and broadcasted, perhaps even across all of infidel America, the moment was too good to pass up. He drew his 9mm Beretta which already had a round chambered. Mary was kneeling, gazing up at him in shock. He stepped toward her, lowered his pistol so that the barrel was nearly touching her forehead.

"Oh, sweet Jesus," she gasped.

He laughed at her pathetic prayer and then squeezed the trigger three times.

As he returned to the car, his companion in the backseat slapped him on the shoulder in congratulations and held up the pad they had with them to monitor how their jihad was going in Austin. The camera was focused straight down on their car, a stream of blood pooling out from under the woman's head, spreading an ugly red stain on the white concrete pavement. A reporter, the woman anchor for the local station, was visible in a side box. It was hard to hear, the rotors of the helicopter pounding the air, but it looked like she was screaming in horror.

He shifted the car, turned the wheel sharply, swinging it onto the shoulder. There was no reaction from any of them as they ran over Mary's body and accelerated.

*Near Portland, Maine*

"Oh God, oh my God!"

The crowd assembled in the recreation room of St. Margaret Mary's Church, of parents with children, husbands and wives under siege at nearby Chamberlain Middle School, had at first shouted protests when the local station in Portland, Maine, went back to the national feed for a moment, which was a live report from Austin, Texas. It appeared that one of the highway killers had been stopped.

Kathy heard the announcement of a feed from Austin, which caused her attention to focus on the television, blocking out the arguing erupting in the crowd. More than a few were actually holding up guns, demanding that they get organized and go in to save their kids. Others shouted back that the police were handling it. The priest climbed up on a table along with the elderly local cop, and barked for everyone to calm down, to have silence so the officer could explain what was happening.

"Live 'Eye In the Sky' Report From Austin, Texas:

Murder on I-35," was bannered across the bottom of the screen and Kathy shoved her way through the crowd for a closer look. Her friend Mary was on that same road.

The camera focused in on the jihadists' car, steam pouring from a shattered radiator, coolant spraying onto the hot engine block.

They actually stopped them in at least one place, was Kathy's first thought and at least for a few seconds, her terror regarding the ordeal of her husband and daughter was subsumed by the desire to see that somewhere, anywhere, the murderous bastards were being thwarted.

Three men leapt out of the car, one running up to the driver's side of a white car.

Seconds later the door opened, the black-clad killer reached in and pulled a woman out.

"No," Kathy gasped, "It can't be her, no."

The woman's long blonde hair was just like Mary's, which she had been so proud of as a young college girl and still sported nearly twenty years later. It was whipping in the downdraft of the hovering helicopter.

A man from the next car in front of the white sedan suddenly fell. The camera zoomed in on the man seizing the sedan and then he actually looked up, face clearly visible, and waved to the camera. The other two were already in the vehicle. The man then turned to the blonde woman who was looking up as if appealing to her killer, or was it to God? And in that instant Kathy did indeed recognize her. It was Mary, it had to be Mary.

She was recognizable for only another second as the man pressed the barrel of his semi auto to her forehead.

"I know her!" Kathy cried, but a second later her beloved college roommate, the friend who had been her bridesmaid, her lovely face disintegrated into an unrecognizable mask of death.

"Oh God, oh my God!" It was the local news anchor screaming, her cries joined by Kathy and others who had paused in their arguing to stand beside her to watch.

The white car, Mary's treasure, a BMW she and Ted had purchased the year before, was now in the hands of the murderers as they pulled onto the shoulder, running over Mary's prone body and then speeding off.

"Cut this feed now!" someone was shouting from off-camera. The local Austin reporter broke into sobs, unable to continue.

She looked back up at the camera, stifling her tears.

"Don't cut it," she cried. "Let everyone see what they are. We will not hide it this time as we did before. Keep that feed open, damn it! Are you seeing this? My God are you all seeing what they truly are? What they are doing to us?"

The Austin news anchor stood up, pointing to someone off camera.

"Do not cut this feed!" she cried.

She was cut though, by the national network which switched back to the studio in New York, the main anchor for the network during this hour, obviously struggling to remain calm. But in a side box, the images from Austin continued to air.

"I agree with her. We are not going to censor what is happening across the nation in this hour of tragedy," his voice trembling.

He paused, pulling off his earpiece to block out the shouts of the program director to not comment further.

"I was embedded with our troops when they went into Iraq in 2003 and saw up close some of the horrors of war, but never anything as we just witnessed. I am asking our teams out in the field, our affiliates in their studios in cities under siege, to remain calm, please stay calm even as you report this nightmare engulfing us."

Stay calm? Irrationally, Kathy whipped her cell phone back out and hit Mary's contact photo. No carrier. She tried a second time, nothing. A third time, and finally it started to ring.

*Near Austin, Texas*

The cell phone lying on the console of the BMW began to ring, the ringtone a popular song in America that summer about being happy, though he did not recognize it. They had just shot up three more cars as they raced along the shoulder of I-35 northbound. The helicopter overhead was following them, his brother in the back seat commenting in Arabic (they were again free to speak openly rather than in the detestable English), how the fools were giving them more than enough warning of police attempting to create a road block up ahead. As he spoke, the camera zoomed out for a quick shot of several civilians armed with rifles lining up on an overpass, complete to a scrolling map marking the GPS locations of the helicopter, of their vehicle, and of the attempted road block.

Three miles ahead there might be serious resistance. Police were running about, pushing civilians out of their vehicles then jumping into them to maneuver the cars to form a complete road block across the entire width of the northbound side of the highway. Civilians were joining them as well and the police were not stopping them now. Men, and, to the disgust of the jihadists, women as well, were pulling out rifles and pistols from their cars and falling in alongside the police.

The training and orientation they experienced before they came here was correct. This was a cowboy state, something like the damned Kurds who were not sheep but tough fighters. It took only a few seconds of the news feed to show that the way ahead was turning into a trap.

The Americans, though, were fools compared to the Kurds, with their need for everyone to be told the latest news up to the second. If not for the news broadcast that they were monitoring on their computer pads, they would have driven straight into the ambush. The driver scanned the side of the road ahead. There was an opening in the highway crash barrier, even a paved crossover lane to the southbound side.

"I'm taking this," he announced in Arabic, slamming on the brakes, skidding to a stop, scraping the fifty thousand dollar BMW against one side of the barrier, cutting across to the southbound side, and turning to now run in the other direction.

His other brother looked at the ringing phone.

"What is area code 207?" he asked.

"I think Boston. Why?"

"Someone named Kathy."

The man holding the phone laughed and clicked it on.

"My God, Mary, are you okay?" a voice cried.

"Oh, so that was her name?" he replied tauntingly.

A pause.

"Who is this?"

"Your bitch American whore friend is dead. We sent her to hell as she cried for your Jesus."

Kathy actually recoiled, pulling the phone back, gazing at it, the horror of the seconds before transformed into rage. "Burn in hell, you bastards. We'll kill you all!" she screamed.

There was laughter on the other end, so enraging that she threw the phone against the wall, shattering it. To merely speak to one of them, to curse them without any hope of effect, filled her with disgust. Even as she destroyed her phone she raged at herself. She had cut herself off from reaching out to Bob and Wendy.

Those around her turned to look at her.

"I was talking to one of them!" she cried, breaking into sobs and pointing at the television screen. "That was my friend you saw killed. I spoke to the bastard who killed her. God, where is God?"

The parish priest pushed his way through the crowd as she started to collapse, grabbing hold of her.

"What happened?"

"That woman on the television. She was my friend," and then she pointed to where she had thrown her phone against the wall, shattering it. "My God, I spoke to her killer just now. He laughed, he just laughed."

The priest drew her into his embrace.

"Let's pray, please let's pray."

"Nooo! I want my husband, I want my daughter…"

She broke free and pushed her way through the crowd to the door.

*Near Austin, Texas*

The three jihadists resumed their mission. The one with the broken arm took on the job of grabbing the weapons that were emptied, handing back one that had a fresh magazine. In less than the hour that they had been engaged, their supply was beginning to run low. They had fired off nearly three quarters of their ammunition in the gleeful opening moments of their killing spree.

He shouted a warning to the other two. They had less than four hundred rounds left. It was time now to make every shot count. One shot, two at most, to kill as they had been trained.

He had a second job as well, one given to all of them in case an injury incapacitated his ability to fire a weapon accurately. He was to have a pad up, Blue-toothed to miniature cameras on their headbands, and monitor the sending of the live video to receivers back in Syria and ISIS-controlled Iraq. Receivers who, within minutes, would turn it around for upload to the internet.

Within minutes their glorious accomplishments would be fed to hundreds of millions who would cheer them on and offer prayers to Allah for their continued success. Surely with so many praying for them, Allah's shield would bring them even greater triumph before the last bullet was fired.

The killing here had become absurdly easy. The southbound lanes had come to a near crawl. The Americans called it "rubber necking." The fire from the truck carrying acetone which had burst into flames on the northbound side had stalled traffic. It was now a matter of simply driving along at little more than twenty miles an hour and popping a couple of shots into each car they passed. The local news feed dutifully reported that they had reversed direction. Cars ahead of them were slamming to a stop, drivers and passengers leaping out and running.

They had been warned, and received extra training over the fact that this was the American state of Texas. It was filled with cowboys and therefore they expected to face more opposition than the far more tamed sheep that other teams were facing in states such as Connecticut, New Jersey, New York, California, and most of New England.

A bullet suddenly shattered the passenger side window, the .45 caliber round nearly striking the driver. He cursed, pointed out the cowboy who was shooting at them: a man with a heavy revolver braced on the hood of his Ford truck. The jihadist in the rear seat, expended half a magazine of rapid fire to bring him down. There was a cry of exaltation.

Another cry of delight escaped as they came upon a bus trapped in the traffic. They emptied an entire clip down its length while their wounded loader scolded them to conserve ammunition. Nevertheless, they made sure to capture both the bus and the cowboy on video.

Up ahead, the pad's news feed was showing that the police they had blocked off earlier when they struck the truck that exploded into flames had been alerted to their approach and were running across the highway, the fools in the helicopter news camera keeping pace with them to capture the potential road block and film their demise. There were essentially trapped on this stretch of road.

The camera shifted from the highway back toward Austin. A Blackhawk was approaching. It looked military. Would they use it? With their American obsession of avoiding injuring their own and even avoiding injuring civilians on the ground in Iraq and Afghanistan, would they actually use it?

The noose might be tightening but the mayhem, the glorious attack, would continue on to the bitter end. He switched the camera on the pad so that his face could be seen.

"Allahu akbar! The infidels are dying like sheep waiting to be slaughtered."

# CHAPTER SEVEN

*Near Raqqa, Syria*

There was a wild exaltation in the room, a well-concealed bunker created beneath a mosque on the edge of that war-tortured city. It had been activated that morning as the nerve center for this day. A pad, Blue-toothed to a flat screen mounted on a concrete wall, was the active receiver of the moment for twitter account *#diesirae631*. The messages were scrolling across the screen so fast that at times they could hardly be read. *#diesirae654 Allahu Akbar, many infidels now in hell, school burning. #diesirae673 our killing police on their national news Allahu Akbar... #diesirae654... #diesirae644... #diesirae627...*

All were proclaiming victories, boasting, joyous with how easy the killing was, as he, their leader, had promised it would be. Before the last of the jihadists died, the Americans would be tearing themselves apart yet again, screaming at each other to change the document that some worshipped as if it were a God, regarding their right to buy and carry guns while others would scream about the source of some of the weapons which dated back years to a surreal plan by their own government. It would be one of many additional benefits of their attack that he had spoken of to his inner circle.

Several other screens in the room showed live feeds coming straight from the jihadists traveling the highways and from the schools under attack. The technologies of the infidels were being turned against them.

A broadcast from Austin, Texas, coming from one of their major networks showed his team there shifting vehicles after their first one was disabled by police fire.

His fighter actually made a point of arrogantly and cheerfully waving to the camera before executing the American whore who had owned the high-priced German car. The mere fact that the blonde was allowed by her husband to drive a vehicle on her own was a clear enough sign to all of the moral decadence of the enemy and, for that sin alone, she deserved the punishment received. He hoped her husband saw the just result of his spineless folly.

A feed sent by his team assigned to Interstate 75 working south from Valdosta, Georgia, were enjoying an absolutely open killing ground on the broad highway, traveling at over one hundred and sixty kilometers per hour on the flat open interstate, having already left behind them a hundred kilometers of wreckage.

The signal had gone dead from the teams assigned to Interstate 40 in North Carolina and the Knoxville, Tennessee, area. The final video sent from the Knoxville unit was of their approaching an overpass where at least half a dozen armed men and women were waiting, firing down on their vehicle. In contrast, on the Interstate 91 going north along the Vermont, New Hampshire, border, the holy warriors were having a joyful killing spree.

The team assigned to the tangle of interstates southwest of Boston at the 495 and 95 interchange were now caught in a massive traffic jam, had finally abandoned their car and were simply walking among the vehicles, executing trapped drivers who, sheep-like, were too terrified to get out and run. They were reporting that once they saw an opening they'd grab another car and continue their run toward Rhode Island.

All of this information was flooding in, along with the news media feeds from the United States. Their major networks were now reporting that cell phone networks were overloading and going down, and the most popular internet social media site servers were overloading as well. The fact that millions could not cling to their crutches of cell phones and social media was increasing the level of panic.

He laughed at that one. Every American was so self-centered that he viewed his own slightest crisis as an emergency, ready to call 911 if he spilled a cup of hot coffee on himself. In their panic they would not listen, jam the highways, and the chaos would continue to spread.

When ISIS released their one-hour video back in June of their triumphal advance into Iraq, the reaction in the West had been fascinating and revealing. All of the American news media sources, both general broadcast and print, had picked up on it within an hour. But then they censored it. They culled out excerpts: the execution of several dozen traitorous collaborators lined up in a ditch, the individual executions with a pistol to the back of each man's head, a ten-year-old hero shooting several traitors, all of it was censored. Their media would show the moment leading up to the kill, but then stop there. Far too upsetting for the infidels with weak stomachs to see. They might become ill and switch to their favorite reality show rather than see their fate if they did not submit to the will of Allah.

The media prefaced the brief clips that they did show with words such as "an alleged execution near Mosul," "a purported execution," a "supposed execution." It was as if the film that his organization had created had its own Hollywood special effects team at work to fake the actually killings. How the Americans loved their fake violence in their perverted movies of sex and killing, but could not stomach it for real.

They could not hide what was happening now. Their

technology had leapt forward in the years since September 11. Every one of their citizens was armed with a cell phone camera and instant access to the entire world. In less than two hours, tens of millions of videos showing the carnage were flooding into the global media, to be forwarded by hundreds of millions more. Allah be praised, they were now wallowing in their terror for the whole world to see. This glorious chaos created by little more than a hundred of his holy fighters.

He had a dozen highly-trained technicians at work in the command bunker. One had been educated at Oxford, another had attended classes at M.I.T. It was a team of expert video editors who, the moment the Sword operations began and the first uplinks flooded in, were sorting through the traffic, capturing the best images and creating near instant, well-crafted media for the global internet. Their productions were designed to instill terror in their enemies and joy for true believers. Even now the first videos were being fine-tuned and soundtracks added, their songs singing of the glory of the prophet, about to be uploaded to news sources across the Middle East and the internet in general.

"We have a good one here," one of his technicians announced and pointed at the screen.

It was a live feed from a news helicopter circling the school near Portland, Maine, where a highly successful attack was taking place. Though there had been a report that one of the fighters had been killed, what one of them was now doing was being broadcasted by the local affiliate and picked up by the national feed. This was the moment that would notch it up even further.

*Near Portland, Maine*

Standing on the roof of Joshua Chamberlain Middle

106

School, one of his courageous fighters was looking up at a circling news helicopter. It was the local Fox station, its logo clearly stenciled on the side, circling tight, camera aimed straight down.

His fighter was holding what looked to be a girl of about twelve years or so who continued to struggle as he held her tight against his side.

And then he did exactly what was done at the school in Chechnya, starting by yanking her skirt off...

*New York City*

"Kill the feed! Kill that feed!"

The New York anchor was out of his chair, screaming to his program director. The huge, oversized screen behind him went dead but the monitor facing him, not visible to the national audience, was still showing what was being done to the young girl, and he stood silent, shaking. The studio went silent; they were not broadcasting the image of the rape, but monitors inside the studio were still receiving the images being sent down from Portland, Maine.

Discipline, the long years of discipline which had held up even during the darkest moments of 9/11 broke inside the studio at the sight of the torturing abuse of the child. Screams of shock, rage, and anguish filled the room. The anchor just stared at the screen, his features going pale, his fists clenched in impotent fury. America was not directly seeing the rape, except in the Portland area where the program director had gone into a state of catatonic shock and had not switched the signal off. But the rest of the world was seeing it nevertheless in the reaction of the anchorman, who stood transfixed, tears streaming down his face.

There was the flash of the knife, held up high so the

circling helicopter could see it, even as the chopper started to dive down toward the roof of the school. The pilot was unable to bear what he was witnessing and decided to land, to try and intervene with his bare hands.

The knife slid so easily across the child's throat, ending her agony.

The anchor, finally aware that he had been standing silent in front of a national audience for a minute or more, looked back at the camera.

"Are we on?" he muttered. "Are we on live?"

"You are, but the video feed is not," a cameraman announced, his voice shuddering.

"The child is dead, thank God," he whispered. "Dear God, we implore You, please still her pain and grant her peace."

He could not speak for a moment, tried to, then knowing he could not control his emotions he lowered his head, his shoulders shaking. He finally raised his gaze to the camera with a cold, icy stare.

"Are we on?" he asked again. A voice off-camera responded that they were going out live, but only from the studio.

"If there are police seeing this, listen to me. In the name of God, end it now. Storm the schools. They are not taking prisoners. They are now raping and torturing the children trapped within. Storm the schools, save our children and then..." He paused. "And then kill every one of the animals doing this. Kill them all!"

He turned his back to the camera, his shoulders shaking as he cried uncontrollably. He knew his appeal to the police had, without doubt, ended his career, but he no longer cared. The image of what he had just seen done to a child...? If he did not cry out in protest then what kind of man was he?

*Inside Joshua Chamberlain Middle School*

The killer just missed him, bullets peppering the wall mere inches over his head. Bob pretended that he had been hit, went limp, and laid still for long minutes, not daring to move. Shooting continued from down the hallway, but not in his direction.

How long had it been? Bob was feeling increasingly light headed, his mind blanking out, and forced himself to focus. He finally dared to crawl the last few feet to the man he had killed, grabbed the M-4 from his grasp, and pulled out the 9mm strapped to his shoulder harness. He tried not to take in the horror of the classroom. They were all dead, there was nothing he could do here. He could hear long bursts of volleys from the administrative wing and further on from the area of the gym and dining hall.

He decided to try and crawl down the hallway, perhaps ambush one of them from behind. He dragged himself out the doorway, made it half a dozen feet, and then the black, covered head appeared again. The terrorist saw him and fired a burst, a round striking his shoulder and the floor. Bits of torn linoleum sliced his face. He feigned that he was dead yet again, and the gunman turned back to keeping the police outside at bay.

Bob rolled in tight against the wall, kept the M-4 poised and aimed down the corridor. He no longer had the strength to move. Waves of pain from his back and shoulder slammed him every second or so. He sensed that if he tried to get closer, they would finish him off for certain. But he could still do something. If the teachers in the classrooms behind him had not yet pushed their children out the windows and fled, if one of the attackers came this way, he would wait until the last second, mimic death, then kill him.

As he waited, the agony continued. He knew that his back was broken. The numbing shock of being hit not just once, but twice, was rapidly wearing off and the pain was building with each passing minute. The damn fire alarm was still screeching and the hallway fire sprinklers still soaking him. So much water was puddling that streams of pinkish slush washed around him. His brain started to register the heavy scent of spent gunpowder overlaying the metallic smell of blood.

One child, about twenty feet away, was curled up, shot in the stomach, and sobbed softly, calling for her mother. He managed to get her attention, motioned for her to lie low and to be still. He recognized her; she was one of his daughter's friends.

"Help is coming, Jessica, just be quiet so they don't shoot you again."

She nodded and, biting her lip, she remained down.

Something outside sounded different and was getting louder. Was it a helicopter? It was thundering, as if it was directly overhead on the roof above.

My God, they're doing something at last!

Then a long burst of shots sounded, followed by a loud crashing blow. Part of the roof above buckled as a chopper blade cut into the ceiling. Then there was a deafening whooshing explosion. The floor and walls shuddered. It felt like the building was about to collapse all around him. All went still. A trickle of burning jet turbine fuel began to rain down through a rent in the ceiling. From outside came a rising barrage of gunfire. The gunman out in the hall fired long, sustained bursts and shouted over and over the cry that Bob now found so sickening: Allahu akbar!

Though the national network had cut the feed from

110

Portland, the local affiliate had not. And so the images of the horror played out on the roof continued to be broadcasted to the local community. It was followed by the crash of the helicopter which burst into flames, a final dizzying shot from inside the chopper spun around, then the signal was cut.

Police had been monitoring the broadcast as well. The dead officers outside the building had created the effect the murderers wanted. They had caused the responders to pause, evaluate, and wait for backup and the SWAT team to arrive from Portland. But the sight of what transpired on the roof had pushed them over the edge. A dozen officers, on their own and with no leadership, broke cover to charge the building. All died on the front lawn.

Kathy recognized the terrified face of the child. The girl lived, or had lived, just down the street. She was someone who, though a grade younger than her own Wendy, liked to hang around with "their crowd" of girls. That could have been her Wendy and now she, and everyone else in the room, truly snapped.

The recreation hall became a sea of bedlam, the shock compounded when the concussive blast from the downed helicopter rattled the windows.

Without the urging of any one individual, nearly all turned to the door and stormed out. There was no leadership, no direction, no plan. Each parent was filled with rage and terror. Nothing, no police line, no reasoning for calm, would stop them now. For that matter, the local police who were trying to maintain some semblance of crowd control while the professional SWAT team from Portland deployed out, were swept up as well. It was their children in there. If not their children by birth, nevertheless they were their kids.

Kathy ran with the crowd, tripping and stumbling, then was up again. They surged back to the main approach to the school, which was still jammed with stalled and abandoned cars.

*The White House*

"This is definitely the Dies Irae attack that we discussed back at the staff meeting in August."

The room was silent with that.

"A statement will have to be made."

There were nods of agreement. The press room down the hall was in chaos, jammed with every reporter who had a press pass and was already on the grounds. In the name of national security, every federal office, including the Capitol and White House were now in full lockdown. No one other than a designated few would be permitted to enter and no one was to leave. Panicked appeals of the staff on Capitol Hill and the White House of the need to get to their children's schools and get them the hell out were met with the assurance, which was in fact true; that any school in the D.C. area and outer suburbs that had children whose parents were high-ranking officials had already been secured.

That scenario of protective response, at least for the children of those working the inner corridors of Washington D.C. had, of course, been thought out and planned years ago. The Quaker school, behind its most peaceful façade, was 24/7/365 a heavily armed and protected camp, even at two o'clock on a Sunday morning, to ensure no one could ever slip in to plant an IED. The President's children had already been evacuated out, airlifted up to Camp David just in case. Just in case there was an additional component to Dies Irae that might involve the White House itself.

112

As for all the other children in the various private schools within the nation's capital and out in the suburbs, the best of highly trained security personnel had already, in some cases, been airlifted in by helicopter.

The Press Secretary was sent out to calm and reassure and to announce that once the extent of the crisis was fully realized and resolved, only then would the nation's leader speak.

# CHAPTER EIGHT

*Near Raqqa, Syria*

"Do we cut it or keep it for this next upload?" the head video editor asked, looking away from his control board to their caliph.

The caliph looked around the room. It was not his nature to seek the advice and opinions of others, or to have someone publicly question him in such a manner. He felt that his four years in an American prison in Iraq had given him an intimate understanding of his most hated foes. But he could hear caution in the video editor's voice, the one who had actually gone to America to be educated, had actually married an American-born woman, at least of a Lebanese Muslim family, whom he had divorced shortly after the call of jihad spurred him to return to his roots.

"Why do you ask?"

"For our own fighters yes, the footage of the child is priceless," was his first reply. "Some though, their hearts are not yet as hardened as ours."

The way the young man asked the question, he sensed, was carefully chosen. He wanted to make it clear that it did not trouble him; it was an act even sanctioned by clerics of their faith. The child was older than one of the brides of the prophet, and being an infidel, she had no protection under holy law, her rape was legal and an act she deserved. That she was infidel trash placed no sin upon the jihadist who did it. They had discussed doing thus, as their brothers had done on the roof of the school in Chechnya to terrorize the infidel Russians, both Orthodox and atheist. So why this questioning now?

"Explain."

"Our target audience in the first releases of our video

reports are of our own faith."

His gaze in reply to that response carried a warning. Most of the Sunni were weak in their faith but still, they were Sunni. The Shi'ite, the enemy dating back across thirteen centuries with their false doctrines, were effete Persians who must be subdued.

"Go on."

"What the West calls the moderates, they claim that they are followers of the prophet, praised and blessed be his name, how will they react to this now, today? The footage we have so far, we want them to rejoice, to celebrate in our victory. But this…"

He pressed a button on a control board for the video editing, winding back to the moment when the jihadist had begun to pull the clothing off the struggling girl before pinning her down.

"The westernized ones will recoil, infected as they are with the teachings of the West. They will be fearful to cry out loudly in praise of what we are doing today."

He pointed to an image of the rape.

"This might sicken some of their leaders who do not have the faith that we have."

"Therefore?" he asked.

"Leave it out for now. The destruction of the helicopter with an M4 is a coup, along with the exploding trucks on the highways. I have that ready to go with our next upload, but I ask for your sanction not to include this particular scene for now."

"Later?"

"Of course."

He was silent for a moment, all eyes of his staff focused on him.

"Do so," he announced and turned away.

Three minutes later the video editor posted up the

116

second release, a carefully edited montage of images and clips, garnered from their own fighters and from the terrified response of America's media, which was now including hysterical reports that were flooding onto the pages of Facebook and other social media. In less than five minutes, the video montage was going viral.

Newer images were inundating their bunker complex, including, to their delight, the first reports of Americans venting their anger on innocent Muslims: a report of a drive-by shooting of a sacred mosque in Dearborn, Michigan, an attack on a small group gathered outside a mosque in Washington D.C. A traditionally liberal news media source was already interviewing an "expert" who was proclaiming that their faith was peaceful and attacked the racists in America, shouting angrily that he had received a report of a lynching in a Somalian neighborhood in New York and several shops being burned. Of course there was no footage other than that of New York City police protecting the shops allegedly under attack. That didn't matter, the voice-over with translation would state that the police were killing the owners of the shops.

The effect that they had sought was already taking hold in Gaza, with thousands pouring into the streets in joyful celebration. Ultimately the celebrations would trigger the Zionists to react, and in so doing provide more video for them to selectively use.

The impact was infinitely greater than on 9/11. Rather than just final frantic phone calls made to loved ones before circuits jammed up, it was live video feeds recorded only seconds before the one recording it died.

One video posted to a social media site was particularly effective: the twelve-year-old boy who had started to send it was dead. He had been filming the entryway to his classroom and whispering to his parents that he was still alive and waiting for help. The door burst open and the boy actually recorded the shot that killed him. His cell phone, clutched in his dead hand, continued to film, showing the shattered classroom, the dead bodies, and the sound of gunfire in the background.

Messages were going the other way as well. Parents reached out to their terrified children, praying with them, and whispered reassurances to darkened closets and hiding places that help was coming.

In three of the schools, the jihadists managed to herd hundreds of children into the dining area or gym, as was done in Chechnya, and started to open the sham of negotiations, releasing a young child every fifteen minutes or so, and offering trumped-up demands about the release of prisoners in Iraq, Israel and America in exchange for the surviving children. They threatened that if any attempt was made to infiltrate the building, all would be slaughtered. That was the plan anyway, but the Americans always fell for such offers.

Another part of their plan had worked superbly well: the fake IEDs. They had been scattered at the approaches and doorways leading into the schools. In the three buildings where hostages had been herded together, the terrorists made a big show of mounting small bundles with cell phones duct-taped to them onto exit doors, basketball hoops and overhead light fixtures. The "explosives" were pointed out to all huddled together, lying or sitting on the gym or dining room floor, that if any one made one wrong move, or if any attempt to retake the building was made, the packages would be detonated, spraying the room with hundreds of ball bearings that would maim and kill.

There were a few who disbelieved the threat, or clearly saw that there were several dozen adults and only one

118

murderer in the room. Their peers subdued any attempt to resist, in one case even beating down and pushing the one who wished to fight back with fearful cries as the jihadist walked up to him, put a bullet into the young man's head, and announced that he would spare the rest this time, but not again.

One of the teachers, attempting to be reasonable and understanding, actually told the killer that she would cooperate with helping him keep order in the gym as long as he promised not to harm the children. He, of course, agreed with her while she prattled on about her understanding and respect for his religion. He smiled, saying nothing. This whore would get special treatment before she died.

Yes, everything was going according to plan. But a storm was now gathering around the schools. At Chamberlain Middle School, the paradigm was shifting, as it did on Flight 93, as the enormity of what was being done was at last being realized and the reaction began to set in, motivated by panic but also by rage.

# CHAPTER NINE

It was a long quarter mile run to the school. Kathy was gasping for air after the first few hundred yards, a flash thought of how, just a few years back, she could easily run several miles a day. Two thoughts drove her forward: the fact that her daughter and husband were still in that school and the searing images of that rape. She still had her Ruger and she drew it out, noticing that several other parents were carrying weapons as well.

For everyone running toward that building, the rape was what penetrated the full enormity of the attack into their souls. This was no lone psychotic gunman. These were jihadists, news reports were now openly linking them to the murderous ISIS cult. The war that ISIS had promised for months had come to America's shores, to the classrooms of their children. There was no room for negotiations, no hope that this would be settled and some children spared. A primal urge seized all, to risk all to try and save their children. They realized that the years of listening to leaders telling them to be passive, to let others do the protecting, completely unraveled at the sight of what was done to the young girl on the roof of their school. They would have to fight in the same way they had once heard respected grandfathers talk of distant beaches in a long ago war, though this fight was against an enemy even darker than Hitler's SS.

The crowd surged forward.

Kathy could see the fire on the roof of the school, the blackened helicopter lying on its side, coils of thick smoke rising into the startling blue autumn sky. Another helicopter was circling, far higher up now, but continuing to film. Lines of yellow tape had been stretched across the road, linked among half a dozen police cars. Officers stood, several holding up weapons, and turned to face the surging crowd, one of them stepping forward with a megaphone.

"Get back. For God's sake, please get back."

But whom was he to address? There was no one single leader in this crowd of nearly two hundred. Something had snapped, the willingness to meekly obey. Kathy could see her new friend Craig at the head of the group, pointing at the school, yelling, and then just tearing the tape aside. An officer tried to block him and someone shouted that the SWAT team was getting set to go in.

No one listened now. They pushed through and started for the school while the perimeter of officers stood watching, stunned. Only a few minutes earlier a dozen of their comrades had tried to rush the building and had been unmercifully mowed down. They too were sick of waiting.

The senior officer in charge saw the crowd, then, looking back at the pad an assistant was holding with trembling hands, which was showing a repeat of the horror on the roof, knew that all was going beyond his ability to contain or control.

That, and emotion and rage had taken hold of him as well.

"The hell with it. Everyone, we're going in."

The rapist was off the roof, climbing back down the access ladder that he had scaled minutes before. He ran, bent low, to join his brother positioned in the foyer. He actually slipped and fell, the floor carpeted with hundreds of ejected shell casings and slick with water and blood. He got back up and inched forward.

"They are coming now," and he laughed grimly.

These Americans with their Rambo fantasies. The surge was coming forward and spreading out. Both men aimed out the front, firing as rapidly as possible, dropping empty magazines, slamming new ones in, and dozens of parents went down under their hail of fire across the front lawn of the school.

It was absurdly suicidal, so many coming straight at them. A number had weapons out and were firing blindly back. What little glass remained in windows was shattering. The front of the mob dropped, but the remainder was spreading out to the sides of the building. More than a few in the crowd had combat experience from the Middle East or were grandfathers from Vietnam. Though disorganized, they began to dodge to either flank, going to the rear and side exits of the building.

The jihadist blocking the main entryway turned to his brother holy warrior.

"I think several classrooms down that corridor still have vermin in them. Kill them now before it is finished."

His brother nodded, rising.

"One of them is armed. I think he killed Ali and has his gun. I think I killed him. Make sure he's dead."

They exchanged glances, smiled, and kissed each other.

"Tonight in paradise."


Bob had nearly drifted off, but the resurgence of gunfire stirred him back to consciousness. He clutched the stock of the M4 for reassurance. If not for what he felt he still had to do, he wished that unconsciousness, even death would come.

He looked over to Jessica whom he had been reassuring earlier. She was still gazing at him, curled up, clutching her stomach. But her gaze was glassy-eyed. The child was dead.

He began to weep with grief. If only they had come

fifteen minutes earlier, perhaps she could have been saved.

Someone was moving in the hallway. He tried to blink away his tears. It was difficult to focus; the corridor was filled with acrid smoke and mist, the sprinklers still spraying out water.

Who was it?

He could hear sustained gunfire and cries of "Allahu akbar!" Whoever was approaching was doing so crouched down, one arm dragging, as if wounded. He was less than thirty feet away, peering through the gloom. It was near impossible for Bob to tell if he was a friend, a rescuer at last, or one of the terrorists. He felt he should shoot and ask questions afterwards, but old instincts prevailed.

"Over here," he gasped, "who are you?"

The response was near instantaneous. The figure dropped prone and fired several shots at Bob, a spray of water kicking up into his face and a blow striking his shoulder yet again. The figure got up and started to rush toward him.

Bob raised his weapon and squeezed the trigger over and over, saw the man double over, stagger, but then keep coming.

The body armor! Damn it, remember they've got body armor. Only a head shot will stop them.

He raised his aim, pumping out more shots, and finally saw the man drop down onto one knee with a strangled cry, apparently hit. The murderer was less than ten feet away, firing blindly. Bob tried to aim, squeezing his trigger again, just one more shot, then the bolt slammed back and ejected a shell casing but did not cycle in another round. He had fired the entire magazine. Was it enough? He began to fumble for the pistol he had taken from the dead murderer which he had laid by his side, but his movements were far too slow. His killer approached but

124

was moving woodenly, staggering as if drunk, knees beginning to buckle.

I got him, Bob thought, but now he will kill me. His opponent fell to his knees in front of Bob and raised his rifle, aiming it for a killing shot to Bob's head.

"See you in hell you pig," Bob gasped defiantly, satisfied that even though he was about to die, at least he had stopped the bastard from reaching the other classrooms.

The man just looked down at him, gasping "Allahu akbar," and he started to squeeze the trigger.

The teams on the highways from California to North Carolina, and from Florida to Maine were being wiped out.

The one that had been sweeping Interstate 95 between Valdosta and the Florida border had been boasting to their leader of their magnificent run, not knowing it was about to come to its end. The broadcasts picked up by their phones and pads which had been so helpful in providing warning of attempts at road blocks and who was pursuing them, were now playing against them as well.

They saw a traffic jam of cars at an exit a couple of miles ahead, the computer map indicating there was a school just off that exit. More easy targets to dispatch.

There were a couple of police cars on the overpass; they would have to be dealt with but the drive could continue. The killing had been extremely good and between them, they still had over twenty magazines left. The two terrorists positioned themselves at the right side windows, one forward to engage the police and throw off their aim, the other to hit the drivers in the cars tangled up in the traffic jam.

Then, at two hundred yards out, it happened. The news reports of the murderers' progress down the interstate was being monitored as well by civilians and police. When the murderers were less than five minutes away, one of the parents, an Iraq vet, leapt out of his vehicle with an AR-15, shouting for anyone who was armed to help him set up a road block. There were three other veterans by his side in seconds, one of them a grandfather of a student at the school, who had fought street by street as a marine sergeant in the battle for Hue in 1968. He shouted his grandson's name to the vet who had started the organizing, told him to convey his love, and with a cry of "Semper Fi," got back in his truck. The elderly marine backed his pickup truck around to face toward where the enemy would come and other parents fell in behind the barrier of cars, armed with weapons ranging from a .22 derringer to an illegal automatic M-16.

They were ready and waiting.

In the final seconds, the jihadists saw that half a dozen of the cars at the end of the traffic jam were actually turned sideways and blocking the road ahead. One of them, a pickup truck, started to move at a right angle across the highway. From behind the parked cars, over a score of men and women, all armed, stood up, leaned across the hoods and trunks of the cars, and unleashed a hail of fire.

The driver was hit in the throat but he was still conscious and able to see that the driver of the pickup truck had swung onto the road, heading straight at them.

Suicide, for a cause that someone believes in, be it to murder innocents or to defend those who are innocent, could be done by both sides.

The killing along Interstate 75 in south Georgia was at an end. The aging marine had given his life to stop them in a head-on collision.

*Joshua Chamberlain Middle School, Portland, Maine*

The muzzle of the rifle was only inches from Bob's eyes. A deafening bang exploded in the corridor and the man who had raped the child jerked upward, his face shattered, and then collapsed.

The hallway reverberated from the rifle shot and several more rounds slammed into the jihadist as he went down. Bob could hear screaming behind him. Children. Merciful God, did one of them get behind him? What was happening?

He tried to roll up onto his side to look back.

"Don't move, don't move a damn inch!"

He couldn't tell who it was, what it was...? The last terrorist? Or a rescuer at last?

"I'm a teacher here," Bob gasped.

The man behind him drew closer, half crouched, and raised his weapon unthreateningly.

"Okay, okay. Are you hit?"

"My back, I can't move. You shoot that bastard?" and he nodded toward the body several feet away.

"Yeah."

"I got the one in the classroom, behind me. I think there's only one left holding the entry."

"How many total?"

"Three, I think."

His savior reached up to a mike strapped to his shoulder.

"This is Sergeant Roberts, State Police, I'm in the main hallway. Most likely three murderers, as reported. Two confirmed dead. At least one still holding the entrance. Get medics in here now, for Christ sake, there are dozens of kids down!"

He hesitated for a second, breathing in short shallow gasps.

"Side entry secured. Get the medics in that way! I'm going for the bastard in the foyer."

He turned to Bob.

"Stay easy, don't move," Roberts whispered. "We'll get you out of here."

"The kids," Bob gasped, "behind me, are they safe?"

"In six classrooms, I don't think anyone is hurt. They're secured."

Bob broke down and began sobbing.

"Thank God, thank you, God…"

"Rest easy. You covered them. Now don't move," and there was a reassuring hand on his twice-wounded shoulder. He winced from the pain. The man who had saved his life drew his hand back, looked at it, and saw the blood.

Roberts clicked on his mike again, announcing that he was going up the hall to take on the last killer and to push medics in immediately through the side entrances.

"I've got a wounded teacher in the hall who held them off. Killed one of them and stopped a second one. I want him taken care of now!"

It was all going hazy for Bob. In a momentary lapse of memory, he forgot that he was paralyzed and tried to stand up, to stay with Roberts, to at least provide some sort of help. The state police officer moved forward, crouched low, moving fast. Bob could hear splashing behind him, cries, and shouts…

Someone was by his side, kneeling down.

"Bob Petersen?"

He looked back up. He couldn't tell who it was.

"Craig Sullivan, you teach my son."

The man was holding a pistol and looking about wide-eyed.

"Have you seen my boy?"

"I pushed him out a window over there," and Bob nodded toward the room across the hall, "After my daughter. I think he made it."

"Oh God, oh thank God," and Craig began to sob with relief.

After a few short gasps for air, he composed himself enough to say, "Your wife was with me, she's outside."

"Kathy? My God, Where? What is she doing here? She should be home with Shelly!"

"I met her trying to get to the school."

Rifle shots crackled from down the end of the corridor and Craig looked up and, without reply and crouching low, ran into the gloom towards the main entrance. Bob could see shadowy figures and bright flashes. It looked like Roberts was at the corner. There were sustained bursts of fire, Roberts was staggering backwards, but he continued to fire.

Then, a moment of silence. Roberts backed up, wavering like a tree about to fall, and lowered the muzzle of his rifle toward the body on the floor in front of him. He fired continually until his magazine was emptied. Then there was silence, though only stretching into seconds, it seemed an eternity to Bob.

"It looks clear!" someone finally shouted.

"Demolition and medics only, get in here now!" another cried. "There are IEDs all over the place!"

He could see several more people dashing through the front entry hall, crouched low, weapons raised. He felt a flash of fear. Were there indeed more lying in wait for the rescue teams to come in?

He heard several more shots, then cursing, then someone yelling that they were firing on their own people.

Someone was slowly walking back toward Bob. It was Roberts; his left arm was hanging limp and the M4 dangled across his chest, still attached to its sling.

Roberts half knelt down, grimacing.

"Your name?"

"Bob Petersen."

"I'm getting a priority medic in here for you now, we'll have you out in a few minutes."

"No, the kids first."

Roberts, struggling to control his emotions, looked about the hallway and then blessedly, the fire alarm stopped shrieking and the sprinkler system shut off.

"Are you certain you saw only three?"

"Yeah. I was in the faculty lounge, saw them rush the front entry. It was three, I'm certain."

As he spoke, Roberts repeated the words into his shoulder mike.

"And you got one? How?"

"I shot him. They have body armor, I shot him in the face."

"You shot him?" a bit of doubt in his voice.

"I had a gun on me."

"How's that?"

Bob hesitated. So strange this moment. He was about to admit to a crime that could land him in prison for five years.

"I always carried a Ruger with me to school, knew this would happen some day and it did."

There was a pause on Robert's part, then he reached out and put a reassuring hand on Bob's shoulder, this time gently and in an almost fatherly fashion.

"This is the second one?" and he nodded toward the body that lay before them.

"I think I hit him. Had the rifle I took from the first one, that was after he shot me. Think I'm paralyzed. Tried to hold the hallway. You got him. Thanks."

"You slowed him down enough for me to finish it, otherwise he'd have been in the next classroom full of kids."

"The kids behind me, are they safe?"

"All of them. You did good, Bob."

"My phone. I think it's still in my shirt pocket. Call my wife, Kathy, tell her I'm okay, and that our daughter got out of the building. She'll be worried sick."

Roberts took the phone out and looked down at him.

"Will do, once we get a back board on you. Okay?"

He could not reply, the world was starting to fade out again.

"I've got a priority here!" Roberts cried. "Back broken, bring a board. Get to him now!"

Bob did not hear that. He had done his job as a teacher this day and he could now let go at last.

# CHAPTER TEN

*New York City*

"We are receiving a report that there has finally been a break with the school sieges. The school just outside of Portland, Maine, Joshua Chamberlain Middle School, the site of that horrific crime on the roof, has been secured.

"Steve Bruce, a reporter with our affiliate there on the ground, is reporting in via cell phone. The signal is not good. As you probably know by now, cell networks across the country are overloaded so it's possible that we may get cut off.

"Steve can you hear me?"

A flickering image was on the big screen behind the anchor. Steve was holding his earpiece with one hand, nodded, then turned his phone around to show the front lawn of the school. A score or more bodies carpeted the ground and ambulances were pulling up on the lawn. Law enforcement personnel were trying to form a cordon, shouting for people to stay back, that the building was rigged with explosives.

"I think you can see and hear what is going on here," Steve began. "About fifteen minutes ago a rush of civilians and police was made on the building, spurred by what happened on the roof."

He raised his phone to scan the roofline, the tail rotor of the crashed helicopter leaning over the side drunkenly, the aircraft burning fiercely.

"That was our station's news chopper. We fear that both the pilot and cameraman are dead."

He paused then pointed his phone back toward the main entryway.

A SWAT team was, at last, dashing in, weapons raised,

a heavy truck pulling up behind them, more personnel getting out.

"We believe that's the bomb disposal unit from the city of Portland. We monitored a request for bomb disposal teams from the naval base in Portsmouth and they are en route by air. I overheard that it might take hours to clear what are dozens of small but deadly IEDs that the terrorists scattered throughout the building.

"Emergency medical teams are going in anyhow, in spite of the risk, to start evacuating the wounded children and teachers."

As he spoke he was herded back farther from the entryway, someone shouting there was a live bomb in the lobby, only a few feet away.

"We've been ordered back. I don't know if you are seeing this."

"We can see it, Steve, just keep talking."

"Oh God, oh God, several people are running out of the building. They look like parents who had been part of the crowd that charged the building. Oh God, they're carrying bodies of children. I can't show this, I can't."

A woman, zombie-like, was walking past him, sobbing and clutching a bloody limp child to her breast. A police officer rushed up to help her, putting himself between her and the building. A medic tried to take the burden from her arms, but this caused her to fight, to scream, and to hold the body tighter.

The world could hear her screaming but could not see it. It was a reflection of the anguish that hundreds were discovering at this moment, that would soon reverberate into the thousands, and then into the tens of millions more filled with empathy.

It sounded like Steve Bruce was arguing with someone. The camera's image moved and he was past the security line, a cop having let him through but saying it was at his own risk. The image came into sharper focus.

It was a woman, clutching a child to her side, announcing that she was a teacher. Someone from another news crew was already focused on her.

"I'm Margaret Redding. I'm a teacher here," she cried. "When it started I ran out into the hallway, saw this child, grabbed her and we hid in a closet. Thank God I was at least able to save this child as we were trained to do."

Steve turned back to face the cameraman who had joined him.

"One of our camera people is with me now. We're told we can get closer but there is still the risk of explosives. It's confirmed that at least six classrooms filled with students were secured in the opening minutes of the attack. Authorities are having them stay in place until the IEDs are disarmed so that they can be safely moved, though medical personnel and a security team are now getting into those rooms."

"At least some good news there, Steve," the anchor replied.

The image suddenly was pointed to an empty sky, and there were loud cries around Steve.

"Steve, what is going on there?"

"Don't want to show this," his voice was breaking again. "A number of parents…"

He paused.

"Oh God," again a pause. "Parents rushed the building, some of them armed. A number of them are dead outside the building, I do not want to show that. Medics are checking them now, some appear to be alive. Some of the parents and police officers were able to gain the building in the rush and are coming out now, having found their children… This is too much to bear."

A pause.

"Turn that damn camera away," and Steve was stepping in front of the lens. A voice, the cameraman, was apologizing, agreeing. Images leaked from the side of the screen where Steve's body was not blocking it: a police officer was collapsing to his knees, rocking back and forth, and crying, "It's hell in there, it's hell, they're all dead..."

Steve forced the camera lens up to focus on his face.

"It's bad here, very bad, I can tell you they are not all dead, I've seen some children come running out in the moments after the final rush started. They are bringing some out now who are wounded.

"I see a stretcher team. It's an adult; he's strapped to a back board."

Steve broke eye contact with the camera, turned his back to it, and shouted a question. A state trooper, wounded and clutching his left arm, approached.

"He's a teacher," the officer announced, nodding back to the stretcher team, "He blocked a hallway and killed one of the attackers and held off another. The man's a hero."

For a nation that needed heroes, the news media now had a focus and Steve told the cameraman to follow him to the stretcher. The stretcher team had put their burden down on the ground. EMTs were working a plasma and medication line into the man's arm, securing a neck brace, hooking up a pressure cuff and electronic leads to monitor his vitals, and leaning over the man, whispering assurances. He was looking about, glassy-eyed, squinting under the afternoon sun after the hours trapped in the smoke and gloomy mist of the school.

"He broke the law!" someone shouted. The cameraman turned toward the woman who had led the child out. "He had a gun inside the school against the law. Someone arrest him now!"

Confusion erupted around Margaret Redding. An officer came up to her, asking her to explain. Margaret shouted that because Bob had broken state and federal law, had defied the training procedures of the school, more children had died, and the results were his fault. But she was engulfed by angry parents shouting back.

"I'll see you in jail, Petersen!" Margaret cried.

"James, turn back here, damn it!" It was the reporter Steve, forcefully pushing the cameraman to shift back to where Bob lay, medics working frantically to stabilize him.

The police officer near the doorway, who had gone into hysterical collapse, was being led away by comrades. Numbed parents and dazed children, who had managed to feign death by remaining perfectly still as their mothers and fathers had coached them to do if ever a "bad man" came into their school, were starting to come out now, but the camera stayed focused on the team that was working to stabilize Bob before loading him into an ambulance.

"He's an incredible hero," it was Roberts, "and to hell with what that damn woman said about the law! He had a pocket Ruger. A lousy pocket-sized gun with maybe six bullets in it against all their firepower and he dropped one of them cold and mortally wounded another. If not for him, we'd have a hundred more dead children in there. In there, my God."

Robert's attention drifted, overwhelmed by the memory of what he had seen inside the building.

"Don't go in there, no one should see what is in there..." he whispered, going into shock.

The camera remained focused on Bob, the cameraman snapping on a light above the lens. Though it was mid-afternoon, it was hard to see Bob's face due to the shadows of the two EMTs leaning over him.

The bright light in his eyes startled him. Bob winced and tried to turn his head away. Someone with warm hands was holding his neck, preventing him from moving, and whispering to him not to move.

It was difficult to comprehend where he was. The front lawn of the school? He looked up at an EMT leaning over him, a young woman, blood smeared on her face, a wisp of red hair peeking out from under her baseball cap.

"My daughter, her name is Wendy Petersen, do you know where she is?"

"We're sorting it out sir, just remain still as I get this neck brace on you."

"I pushed her out the window by the playground. Can you find her, tell me she's okay?"

"We're taking care of it now sir, trust me. She's okay. If you got her out, the children that ran, they all made it."

He knew that her words were not all true. He had seen too many bodies collapsed on the playground.

"She's wearing a pink scarf."

"I promise I'll look for her as soon as we get you on your way. Now please lie still and don't talk. We're trying to help you. You want to get through this for your daughter, don't you? You've got to work with me for your daughter's sake."

He could see that the young woman was trembling even as she secured the brace around his neck.

She leaned back from her patient, signaling that the neck brace was secured. They already knew he had a bullet hole in his back, it looked like just below his sixth vertebrae. His spinal column was almost certainly shattered. There was a second wound in his shoulder, a bullet or bullets having entered from the top, smashing his rotator cup and shoulder blade. It was so badly mangled it might be a fight to save his arm.

There were no exit wounds, so the bullets were still inside him. No blood frothing up in the mouth, so lungs were intact. She double-checked the straps securing him to the back board. If there was a remote chance that his spinal column was not completely destroyed, there might be a hope of saving some ability to walk. No exit wound was in his lower abdomen so the round had, without doubt, driven bone fragments into his lower abdomen. Chances were that there were multiple punctures of his intestine; it was going to require hours of major surgery to clear him out to prevent the onset of sepsis. He was still alive after more than two hours, so definitely no major artery or vein was hit; otherwise he'd have bled out by now.

She was in awe of him as she and her teammate ran their checks. The wounds were horrific. She had seen over and over while deployed as a National Guard nurse in Iraq that, many times, it was the sheer force of will that had kept a wounded soldier alive. Others just surrendered to the quietness of death. Keep them focused on their loved ones at home, tell them to hang on for them. This man had been motivated to stay alive to protect the kids. She had to keep him motivated, now that his task was complete.

"Tell me your daughter's name again?" she asked.

"Wendy Petersen."

"And you are?"

"Bob Petersen."

"Bob, for your daughter, I need you to fight along with me. Keep with me. You got that?"

He looked up at her, his gaze drifting. Every hospital from Lewiston-Auburn, across Portland, and down clear to New Hampshire would be flooded with hundreds of casualties and the terrible task of triage would have to be applied to more than one. He needed hours of surgery, not tomorrow but now, today.

She used a Sharpie pen to make a few marks on his forehead, indicating that he had received an injection of painkiller. She jotted a couple of coded numbers on a tag that she clipped to his shirt with the same information: time of injections and readings of vitals. Her prognosis, though she was no doctor, and her observations in the field would help the doctors in emergency rooms with their decision-making as to how to prioritize those coming in, and initialed it.

She stood up, tearing off her latex gloves, fetching a fresh pair from her pants pocket but not yet putting them on.

"Get him out of here now!"

"Wendy..."

"Bob, you've got to hang in there. I'll find your girl and personally bring her to you. I swear to God I will."

Her voice was beginning to break. It was a promise she was not sure she could keep, but felt she had to make, and inwardly she prayed that she could return to his side with his daughter... alive.

The four taking care of Bob Petersen's backboard gently started to lift it as she prepared to go back into hell.

"Wait!"

He struggled as if trying to sit up. She looked back at him.

"Don't move, Bob, just relax, we've got you taken care of."

"Wait, oh please wait."

He tried to raise his arm to point and she went back to his side. She had been trained that often the wounded bonded to their first caregiver and were frightened when taken from their side. But he had to be moved up the next step of care while she had to go back to the next victim, then the next and the next. She leaned over and kissed him gently on the brow to offer reassurance.

"Calm, Bob, just chill. Okay?" she whispered soothingly.

"That's my wife. My wife!"

He was trying to gesture to a prone body lying limp and broken on the blood-slick lawn only feet away from where he had been set down for treatment.

"Stop! Oh God, please check her," he begged.

It came out as a strangled cry. He was unaware that the television camera was still focused on him.

The medic who had been preparing to go back in to face the carnage within the corridors of Joshua Chamberlain Middle School, stood up, turned from Bob's stretcher and walked over to the collapsed body on the lawn. She already knew the answer. In that first minute of taking back the building, even before the shooting had stopped, medics, herself included, had gone rushing in to check the fallen outside the building.

They did so heedlessly. They did so knowing that, unlike the traditions that had existed in western civilized society for well over a century or more, those wearing the red cross on helmet or sleeve were not exempt here. On other battlefields, in other wars, to deliberate shoot a medic on the enemy side was an act beneath contempt, an actual crime. But with this enemy, those bringing aid, compassion, a final soothing word and injection to still the last moments of pain, drew fire and were defined as the most tempting of targets to kill. Jihadists were trained to kill them even when far more deadly opponents were attempting to kill in reply. To kill a medic was an act to be praised, for it would help to break the enemy's morale or, even better, trigger an act of angry reprisal that could be used against them in the world's media.

141

The body that Bob was trying to point out had already been checked and left where she had fallen, to be cared for later after those still living could be saved, or those whose dying could be eased, were tended to first. Nevertheless, the medic made the effort to kneel down by the woman's side. The dead woman's eyes were wide open and sightless, the ground beneath her soaked, the blood which had poured from her shattered heart and abdomen beginning to congeal.

The medic made a gesture of putting two fingers to the woman's neck, looked back at Bob and nodded.

"Bob, she's alive, she's alive, we'll get help for her now." Her gaze told the stretcher bearers not to wait around, to get him the hell out of sight of the body of his wife. They lifted him high and started off, Bob trying to crane his head back to look, but the neck brace kept him locked in place.

And Bob knew his young guardian angel was lying, a final glimpse showed the medic lowering her head and placing her hand over Kathy's eyes to close them.

The camera crew focused on that, the reporter stood in numbed silence, those in the studio watching were unable to speak. A nation watched as the medic stood up, hands sticky with yet more blood.

"There are still hundreds of children in there, maybe I can at least find his daughter alive," was all the medic could choke out and then she turned and started for the door, her walk jerky, slow, and swaying. A police officer, crouched low by the door, yelled to her to get through the entryway quickly, there was a hot IED but feet away. She did not pay him the remotest heed and just went on in.

Even as the attacks continued, the killing continued, and the rage built, it was the beginning of a nation in mourning.

# CHAPTER ELEVEN

Over the next hour, the four other schools under siege were freed of their nightmares, if freedom could ever really be achieved after what so many young hearts and souls had witnessed and endured. A nation had seen, on their wide flat-screen TVs and on their hand-held phones, images of the carnage.

Every school in America was in terrified shutdown. The nearly 98,000 public schools in America, along with tens of thousands of private and parochial schools, tens of thousands of day care centers, thousands of universities, colleges, and community colleges, all were in lockdown. The universal sound of that day would be the wailing of sirens. Every local police officer, whether on duty or off, had raced to the schools in their town. For almost all, there was a school with their own children or those of friends and neighbors. County sheriffs raced to protect schools as well, until called to go to nearby interstates where an even greater mass murder was unfolding.

State police raced to the interstates. Their years of looking for drunk drivers, or, in quiet moments, pulling over those going eleven miles over the speed limit, or their being first on the scene of a deadly crash, none of that had prepared them for chasing gunmen armed with AK-47s, joyful in their killing and with no intent of being taken alive.

Across the nation every National Guard unit had been called to mobilize by the second hour, but it would take hours more before the first vehicle rolled out, the first aircraft took to the air. Though some of the first black hawks, armed with 20mm and air-to-ground weaponry, were lifting off.

As for the Air Force units within the continental

United States: the half dozen jets that were actually armed and up on routine patrols or practice drills had, when the extent of the attack was realized, been vectored to respond as if it were another 9/11. They closed in on New York, Washington, and other major cities, circled and remained ready to engage.

As on 9/11, an hour and a half into the attack, the FAA informed all air traffic controllers to order every plane in America to land, warning that any that deviated from a flight controller's orders would be shot down without warning. At this time of day, upwards of three thousand commercial aircraft and thousands of general aviation planes were in the air over the United States. It would take time to jockey each plane into position, to redirect planes bound for O'Hare and order them to LaGuardia, to order any aircraft approach from the Atlantic, the Pacific or the Gulf of Mexico that if it had sufficient fuel, to return back to its place of origin or seek emergency landings in Heathrow, Seoul, and Tokyo.

The ripple effects of fewer than one hundred and fifty jihadists were now echoing around the world, as promised by ISIS and their caliph months earlier. As with so many previous threats by other terrorists, this threat had been received with just a ripple of notice.

Unlike 9/11, this time, aircraft were indeed shot down. A commercial flight, a "puddle jumper," missed its approach to Austin, and a new copilot, still in training, when requested by ground control to switch its transponder code and to swing out southwest of the city until things were sorted out, punched in the wrong code. He entered the 7700 number, indicating that they were no longer in control of the plane, that a terrorist had seized it.

A Texas National Guard A-10 warthog was tracked to the plane with the hapless copilot, his error compounded

144

when the plane appeared to be circling toward the middle school that was still under siege. The pilot of the warthog was ordered to release his weapons and to drop the plane, no matter its location. He did as ordered. Twenty-seven innocent people on the plane and eight unlucky people on the ground died.

Thousands of small general aviation planes were up and about on that autumn afternoon; in the northeast it was exceptional flying weather after more than a week of autumn rains and winds. Though it would seem hard to believe for some, more than a few of these pilots were not yet aware the nation was under attack, flying in airspace where radios were not mandated. Three were shot down by civilians on the ground, who assumed they had to be terrorists if they were still up.

All of this chaos was applauded and greeted with joyful laughter in Raqqa, one of the planners crying out that his prediction was right, that the cowardly infidels would now turn about as rabid dogs, and begin to slaughter each other in their fear and insanity.

The shutdown of the American airspace, within minutes, resulted in the announcement of the closings of British, Dutch and German airports to all international flights going to or coming from the United States. The same occurred along the Pacific rim. In another half hour, the ripple effect was indeed global, nearly every nation announcing that all but internal domestic flights were to land at the nearest airport and hold. News sources around the world were reporting their own woes as tens of millions of nonbelievers lamented how their lives had now become inconvenienced, vacations ruined, business meetings delayed, funerals missed, and family reunions cancelled.

The effect even spread to that new hub of world travel,

145

the wealthy sheikdom of Dubai, which would one day very soon acknowledge the caliphate. This global cascade of events was even better than they had hoped for and revealed yet again the weakness and cowardice of their enemies.

# CHAPTER TWELVE

The attacks along the interstates had hit their climax and the end game was on, the personal end game which every holy jihadist on this mission knew would be the final result. All knew that they would not outlive this day. But oh, how they were praised by their clerics (who were staying safely at home even as they extolled others who died) to the rewards that awaited them in paradise. All that had been denied to them on earth was now moments away in the gardens of paradise. In the brief interludes of killing, they braced each other's courage by boasting to each other of all that would be given to them: the praise they would receive, the slender boys with angelic faces who would serve them and the virginal pure women who would await them. Not like the sluts of America with which more than a few jihadists had entertained themselves for a meager price in the days before this holy day of martyrdom. More than one began to chant sura 52, speaking of promises of dark-eyed virgins, of wine and young boys, laughing with joy even as they died. Everything denied on earth would be theirs for eternity in just a few more minutes.

In the car racing along Interstate 76 northeast of Denver, one jihadist considered the banal and earthly concerns and stupidity of the Nazi SS. Kill enough Jews and you got a trifling medal and promotion to some unpronounceable rank. But in his reality, if you kill enough infidels, if you are a believer in the prophet, you gained the most beautiful virgins of paradise. There was even a laughing argument among the three in the car, one of them dying of wounds, as to whose virgins would be the most beautiful and willing to submit and not cry with pain to their lusts. They spotted a somewhat slow Volkswagen van of the 1960s, occupied by an elderly couple traveling across country who were recreating the honeymoon travels of their 50th wedding anniversary and slaughtered them both while trading accounts of whose virgins would be the most beautiful and willing to accept their desires, no matter what was demanded of them.

It was finally an F-18 out of the Air Force Academy that had been stalking the murderers for over ten minutes, desperately waiting for an open space where no other cars would be hit, until finally under direct orders to shoot regardless of further damage, that placed a round into the black sedan, vaporizing the three within and ending their musings about beautiful virgins and young boys. The shot tragically killed half a dozen innocent people in nearby vehicles as well. After he landed, the base doctor and commanding officer reassured the pilot that if he had not fired, far more would have died. He would never fly combat aircraft again, diagnosed with severe trauma.

The team sweeping Interstate 96 between Grand Rapids and Lansing, Michigan, had enjoyed similar success, slaughtering several hundred until all rifle ammunition was depleted. With the final loads for their 9mm semi autos, they had driven up an exit ramp on the outskirts of Grand Rapids, killed two police officers and seized their patrol car. Their pad map showed a Catholic school only half a dozen blocks away, a target that would be an exceptional finish to it all. With siren wailing, they managed to dodge the confusion of hundreds of parents who had blocked the approaches to the school. Leaping out of the patrol car, they attempted to storm the building. Though they killed several dozen, armed parents and police held the entrance to the school.

The report of this attempt on a school, delivered from a police car, created yet more panic. The murderers on the interstate highways, as a final gasp of hate, were now attempting to reach schools close to interstates, especially Catholic schools, disguised as police, and kill all within. Parents, in a renewed frenzy of fear, moved cars to block all approaches to any school while police begged them to keep some lanes open for emergency traffic with several officers shot by panic stricken civilians.

Reports swept the news outlets of lone gunmen being spotted who were waiting to carjack vehicles and set up a hostage situation. Half a dozen people died and several score were wounded that afternoon, as drivers shot at each other, believing the other was "one of them."

And in more than one city throughout the Middle East the reactions were setting in. Many were silent, many sickened, but more than a few joyful as the "Great Satan," was humbled by ISIS.

*Raqqa, Syria*

Though he had never said so to any of the jihadists before they had left for America, the caliph hoped that several, perhaps even half a dozen, of his warriors would be captured. They would have made such excellent pawns in the months ahead.

He himself had been a prisoner for four years in Iraq. But he had never feared for a moment. It was four years of training, an opportunity every day to observe the enemy. Most of the military police assigned to his prison camp had come out of an American National Guard unit from the New York City area. Many were actually survivors of the World Trade Center as firemen, policemen and medics. Every last one had lost comrades on that day.

So perverted in their thinking, these Americans. He knew that most hated him, and yet even then, many had tried to reach out to speak to him when they discovered he could speak their language. To ask him why? Some had

149

even attempted to convert him and he had played along to learn of their weaknesses.

So he knew their vulnerabilities better than they themselves did.

So far only one of his warriors had been captured, somewhat honorably unconscious. He was taken during the storming of the fourth school. There had been a wonderful display of the West's evil racism to show to the world when, as the unconscious man was carried out and put into an ambulance, a crowd gathered and spat on him, demanding that he be lynched in front of the school where over two hundred children had died at his hands. The same police officers who had stormed the school were now having to defend the captive. He would be a useful pawn in the months to come for they would put him on trial, which could take a year or more. Demands would be made for his release and there would be some who would actually argue for his release and thus further divide the infidels against each other.

All around him laughed as they watched a shouting match on an American network between two members of Congress. Their cherished building was in total lockdown, surrounded by hundreds of security with aircraft overhead. The one politician was demanding immediate vengeance, the other shouting back that now was not the time to overreact.

A noted "spokesman" for whatever cause he could barge his way into, was interviewed on a street corner in New York, and shouted that hundreds of innocent ethnic Americans were now being targeted by angry mobs, in a wave of racial hatred not seen since the days of lynchings in the South.

All of this was amusing but there was still one more result that he knew would soon unfold. He had predicted it to his inner circle of followers. It was what their president would do. Announcements were going up that within the hour, their leader would speak.

# CHAPTER THIRTEEN

*New York City*

"It is now approximately three and a half hours since the first report that America is again under attack. An attack far more broad-reaching than 9/11 because it strikes at our very heart as a nation and as parents."

The anchor for the network looked haggard, exhausted. Though used to being on camera for hours at a time, his voice was raspy. And it was evident as well that he was having increasing difficulty with emotional control.

The network's afternoon anchor, his stunned reaction while watching the monitor that had been switched off to the rest of the world, was now a moment etched into the nation's memory. The horror of it all did not need to be seen. His reaction, his features, the way his body recoiled from the horror and his cry for vengeance, was shocking to the generations raised since the 1960s who believed that vengeance could never be an act of justice.

There was a time, little more than a generation ago, when the flow of images was controlled by studio executives, producers, political and even sponsor pressures. If the average citizen had filmed something using a hand-held film camera, be it horror or triumph, unless cleared by "wiser heads," the image was never seen. It was years before the impact of a bullet striking a president down was actually seen as film and not just a few still images.

With the advent of the third and fourth generation computers, the ability to hold in one's hand a computer with more power than the top-secret Cray of the defense industry forty years earlier, and the linking of it to every other computer in the world, had completely transformed how all news and information flowed.

Media was the new frontline battlefield for terror.

So even as the network blocked the images of what had transpired on the roof of Chamberlain Middle School, and those hiding in a bunker near Raqqa decided for the moment to suppress it, the images had been recorded, leaked, and sprung across the internet and had created two responses: rage, and a rapidly growing voice to do something, anything, to finally protect the children, no matter what was required or what sacrifice had to be made. The system was broken, they cried, and "things must be changed for the sake of our children!"

The anchor paused to sip from a glass of water, then continued with his summation:

"We have reports from around the nation, but before we go to them, this is what we can confirm with certainty at this moment. We can confirm from eyewitness reports by our own personnel with affiliate stations across the nation, and from the announcements of local and state officials, that five schools were seized starting late this morning eastern time. There are reports of more than two dozen other schools experiencing some form of attack. One appears to be a copycat by a lone gunman, who murdered two school administrators and a police officer before being killed. Other incidents appear to be tragic mistakes.

"Again I urge you, if you are a parent who wishes to hold your child and get him to the safety of your home, please show restraint. If you have attempted to go to your child's school, please wait in areas designated by authorities.

"Now, to the second concern. Even if you could retrieve your child, in nearly every state, officials have ordered all interstate highways to be closed.

154

"That situation is not yet under control. We cannot give you a confirmed summary at this time, though across the bottom of the screen we are now trying to list all locations where we know that terrorists are still active."

The reporter paused, putting his hand to his earpiece, and nodded an acknowledgement.

"We have just received confirmation from our White House correspondent that within the next thirty minutes the President will address the nation. We are standing by for this new development."

*Portland, Maine*

"Bob Petersen?'

Though heavily sedated, he stirred at mention of his name. The emergency room was a scene of chaos. Every bay was filled of course, the wounded lying on gurneys, on the floor, and standing while awaiting treatment. Outside, ambulances, pickup trucks, anything that could transport the injured from the schools and highways were bringing in more casualties.

A harried orthopedic surgeon had given him all of five minutes, written something on another tag pinned to his stretcher, and leaned over to tell him that his case was too complex, that the hospital had been turned into a triage center. He was stable, would pull through, and was slated for an airlift down to a surgical unit in Boston.

Bob had nothing to say in reply. A horrifying memory returned. My God, Kathy was *dead*. Dead! He would never see her again, never speak to her again, never hold her again. Where was her body and where was Wendy? They had deadened his physical pain but unconsciousness would not come. He began to weep. Shelly. Dear God, did Kathy have Shelly with her when she came to the school. Did they all die and I alone survived?

"Let me die," was all he could murmur to the surgeon, who misunderstood him.

"I can't promise you'll walk again, Bob, but you'll get the best treatment in the world in Boston. You are a hero; everyone is talking about you. We'll do everything we can for you. Thank you for what you did. I have a granddaughter in that school and I just found out she's safe."

The surgeon clasped his hand reassuringly, tears welling in his eyes.

"Leave me be," was Bob's whispered reply.

The surgeon, not understanding the reason for his anguish, thinking it was about the contemplation of being paralyzed, which the one x-ray they took revealed was all but certain, whispered that he'd be fine, thanked him again, and instructed the orderlies to wheel Bob out to a waiting area. A helicopter was already airlifting the high priority cases to the Portland airport where ambulance aircraft were expected shortly from Boston.

"Bob Petersen?"

The voice was insistent. He opened his eyes slowly. It was tough to focus.

It was the young medic from in front of the school. Her face was drawn. Where was he again? Was he back at the school after all? Was the doctor a hallucination? The last he had seen of her, she was kneeling beside Kathy and telling him an obvious lie.

They made eye contact.

"Bob, can you hear and see me?"

He tried to nod, but the neck brace kept his head rigid. His eyes widened with recognition.

"Kathy is dead, isn't she?" he breathed.

She nodded, the corners of her mouth turned down and trembling.

156

"Why are you here?"

"I came back with an ambulance of the wounded but I promised to see you again before going back out there."

"Why?"

And then he knew. She had come to tell him that she had found Wendy and Shelly. She was a messenger for the dead.

He tried to turn his head away. Oh, God, no... Just let me die. I can't live without my family. He could hear sobbing and cries of pain and grief pervading the corridors. There was so much tragedy in this world on this day and he wondered strangely, did God hear and see his tears? Or was the universe truly mad and the psychotic creator of murderers was rejoicing at this sorrow and slaughter, rewarding those who had created such pain?

"It's Wendy, Bob."

"I know, I know," he began to sob, his bound body racked by trembling.

"Daddy?"

Was that her voice from heaven, or was she in hell? He turned back toward the medic angel. Tears were streaming down the woman's face. Someone familiar was clutched close by her side. Was it a hallucination? Am I dying and my baby has come to touch my hand as a gentle angel of death to lead me to peace?

"Daddy!"

Wendy tried to break free from the medic's embrace, but the woman restrained her.

"Wendy, sweetheart. Your Daddy's back is injured. He can't be touched, but it's okay to kiss him on the forehead."

"Daddy, I did as you told me..." and, crying, she stepped to the stretcher and kissed him gently, as if he might shatter if she touched him too hard.

"My baby, oh God, my baby, you're safe!" His tears of sorrow turned into tears of relief.

The wailing, the confusion in the corridor stilled for a moment as nurses, doctors, even those awash in their own grief turned to watch this moment of reunion and of love.

"I ran to the woods as you told me to, Daddy," she choked.

She was calling him Daddy again; gone was the arrogant twelve-year-old of the morning, trying to act sophisticated in front of her friends, her father just "dad" who happened to work at the same school. Right now, he was again "Daddy."

"Daddy, I saw Mr. Sullivan and had to tell him." Her faced contorted with painful memory. "Johnnie got shot. I wanted to help him but he told me to keep running to the woods."

Weeping, she buried her head into the medic's shoulder, who pulled her in close, hugging and soothing her.

"The police found her and a dozen other children in the woods," the medic whispered. "They were all from the same classroom, doing what you told them to do. Poor lambs were too terrified to come out. I saw name tags being put on them before being evacuated, and I recognized your last name. I felt I should bring her to you personally."

He tried to still his tears and smile, unable to find the words to thank this angel.

"Daddy, I tried to call Mommy but she isn't answering her phone."

The medic froze, studying Bob's face. She took a deep breath and shook her head in warning.

How could he tell Wendy now that her mother, his beloved and cherished companion in life, was lying dead in front of their school? Why did she come to the school? Why?

He looked up, appealing to the medic. A thought returned, rescuing him from what he must eventually do.

"We have a one-year-old daughter…" and he began to break completely at the thought that, in her panic to reach Wendy and him, Kathy had brought Shelly along.

The medic leaned over Bob, lips nearly touching his ear so that only he could hear.

"Wendy told me she had a little sister. She gave me her cell phone and I called the number listed as home. A woman answered there and said that the baby is safe and sound."

"Oh God, thank you, thank you!" Bob gasped.

"Priority Red Ones, out on to the helipad now! We're taking four more!"

The call rang down the corridor. The medic wiped her eyes, stood up straight, and glanced at the tag affixed to Bob's stretcher.

"That's you, sir."

She held her hand up and shouted for attendants even as Wendy continued to cling to her side.

Two orderlies, both wearing blood-smeared smocks, rushed to the head of the Bob's gurney, and began to gently maneuver it out the door. Wait! Wendy…!

The helipad outside was awash with the thunder of the rotor blades, the sound of them flashing him back to the terror of the helicopter crashing into the roof of the school, the fuel from its ruptured tanks pouring down in the corridor.

"Wendy?!"

The orderlies stopped.

"She's with me, Bob," the angel of mercy was by his side.

"Get him in, move it!"

They were not giving him any more time.

"Wait! Take my hand, Wendy."

She reached out and grabbed it tightly.

"Daddy is going to be okay, I promise you."

She nodded.

"I love you."

"I love you, Daddy," and then her eyebrows rose in fear and she began to cry. "Where's Mommy? I can't find her! She's probably looking for you."

Bob looked up at his guardian angel, struggling to focus, pleading for one more blessing from her.

"Can you please make sure Wendy gets home?"

The medic reached for Bob's hand and squeezed it.

"Of course," she pulled her hand back and used it to brush tears from her face.

"You may have to be the one to say it," Bob sighed, his gaze drifting from the medic's eyes to Wendy.

"I know," she looked down at the floor and pulled Wendy in closer.

He tried to smile in reassurance, grateful beyond words to this young woman who had come miraculously to his family's aid.

"You give me belief again that there is a God," Bob whispered, as the airlift team checked the tag on Bob's stretcher, then gently lifted him and strapped his gurney into the chopper.

He caught a last glimpse of Wendy in the doorway, held back by the medic. She turned and buried her face into the medic's side, her shoulders shuddering.

That was his last glimpse of the two. As the helicopter left the ground, he finally let go. He allowed himself to weep, to remember, to mourn all that was lost. His whole world, which eight hours ago had started so tranquilly and routinely, was shattered forever.

He did not know the name of the guardian angel who clutched Wendy to her side but knew that she would take her home, tuck her and Shelly in, guard them through the night, and be there with the coming of dawn to comfort their tears. For such were the souls of so many, even now, even when evil stalked the land.

# CHAPTER FOURTEEN

*3:45 p.m., the White House*

"Mr. President, fifteen minutes."

He looked up at his press secretary.

"How is it out there?"

"A madhouse, sir."

He nodded and looked down at the sheaf of executive orders that needed his signature to make them official. The man assisting him, who had been the loudest voice urging this decision, stood silent now. Some staff in the room had vehemently disagreed. Two, both of the Joint Chiefs of Staff who should be present, were not. They had "resigned," one actually doing so, the other ordered to do so.

He recalled the words of a politician who had said to "never let a crisis go to waste."

*Raqqa, Syria*

Word had come in, as it had to the entire world, that their president was about to address his nation in fifteen minutes.

He felt a serene confidence now. Though it was not the appointed hour, he knelt in the direction of Mecca, all in the bunker following his example, and led them in prayer. He had been taught since earliest childhood to serve his god, however harsh the commandment. In a way, this was not a time for rejoicing; it was a time for prayer and contemplation. He had sent more than a hundred of his brothers to their deaths this day and they had done so gladly, obeying the truths that Allah had revealed to him.

He had become the sword of Islam this day unlike any had seen in a thousand years and the responsibility was a heavy one. After the ritual of prayer was done, he remained kneeling in silence, forehead touching the bare concrete floor. He prayed that the enemies of Allah, who were therefore his sworn enemies, would now take the next step, to react as he predicted. For if they did so, what would follow would truly be the beginning of the end times and he would be the instrument of the fulfillment of prophecy. If they took this next step as he predicted, they would then surely turn against themselves as a rabid dog in its death agony bit its own wounds. And then his caliphate would be recognized by all, for in answering Allah's will, his blow had become the beginning of the end of the great Satan.

The moment was nearly at hand. If his enemy did not react as predicted, today was still a great victory. If his enemy did as expected, the victory would eventually become complete.

He will have served the will of Allah and his place in history will be forever assured. His reward in paradise, given to him personally by the prophet, would be the greatest one of all.

At this moment, a televised program out of Riyadh, rather than be a mouthpiece of that corrupt government which believed it held the keys to Mecca, was now so frightened as to move toward a middle road. They were saying that the attack on America must be understood, after so many centuries of abuse and corruption inflicted upon them by the West, dating back to the crusades.

In minutes, all would understand his wisdom, his far deeper insight into the enemy than bin Laden ever had. The American world had changed profoundly in the decade since 9/11 and in a direction few had foreseen. It was a new and vastly different generation of leaders there now. They had become a nation divided, mistrustful of each other.

Already, even as the last few minutes ticked down for this final fulfillment of his plan, their media was laying blame against each other, demanding changes to their laws in order to "protect our children."

Only he and a small handful knew that the enemy had seen more than enough indicators of what was unleashed this day. He knew what they would do and it would fundamentally change them… and then destroy them.

It was 4:00 p.m. in Washington D.C. All in the room fell silent, watching the monitors that were linked to feeds from around the world.

*4:00 p.m., Washington. D.C.*

"Ladies and gentlemen, the President of the United States."

The single camera set in the oval office came on. He was dressed in a dark jacket, white shirt and dark tie, carefully selected by his advisors to convey a somber mood, as if he were chief mourner at a national funeral.

The curtains were drawn behind him. Two flags, the flag of the United States and that of the President of the United States, were the only bright colors in the framed image.

He gazed straight at the camera, hands neatly folded on several sheets of paper resting on the desk.

"My fellow Americans. Today is a day of national tragedy, a day of national mourning, a new day of infamy. Our nation was attacked in the most brutal and despicable way. The images we have seen this day, we will never forget. And we should never forget. Our children have now become the victims of a hateful and villainous plan to create chaos and to frighten us.

"Today must also become a day of national strength.

165

We must remember who we are, what we stand for, and stay strong in our resolve to not be cowered and to remain good and decent people.

"I am disappointed to report that the fighting continues in a number of locations."

He paused.

"And, tragically, fighting now rages among ourselves as well. There have been incidents across America of a spreading violence that is misguided, misaimed at the peaceful and innocent because they share a particular faith.

"Therefore, I have signed the following executive orders."

He paused, lightly tapping the sheets of paper on his desk.

"I have signed a document declaring that the United States of America is in a state of national emergency. Therefore:

"I have ordered the closing of all interstate highways until further notice. This is for your safety and to facilitate the movement of emergency vehicles and troops to secure order.

"I have ordered the closing of all schools, public and private, until further notice. This is to ensure the safety of our children. I leave it to state authorities the decision as to when the lockdown of schools shall be lifted and children released to the care of their parents. If you are listening to me from a secured area near your child's school, once you have your child, you are to proceed home immediately.

"I have ordered a curfew effective at 8:00 p.m. starting this evening, to begin within each time zone at that hour. You must be off the road and in your homes by 8:00 p.m. local time. If you cannot reach your home, seek a safe place to stay. Travel after that hour until 8:00 a.m. tomorrow morning will result in immediate arrest. For your safety and for the security of our nation, you must comply with this temporary restriction.

"Regardless of individual permits to carry a weapon according to various state and local law, I have ordered that the carrying or use of any firearm will result in immediate arrest until such time as this emergency has ended. In light of the tragedies that have transpired this day with attacks upon innocent civilians, the reasoning for this is obvious.

"And finally…"

He tried to offer a reassuring smile.

"Our enemies have used the internet and our computerized systems of communication to coordinate their attacks and commit violence against our citizens. Therefore, I have ordered the immediate suspension of the use of the internet by all citizens until further notice. If you are currently using the internet to communicate with others, you must sign off once this broadcast is completed. The internet is to be reserved for transmission and postings only by designated government officials and agencies in order to provide national security until this crisis has passed. You may continue to monitor the internet for official announcements via approved sources that even now are being listed, but to transmit information of any kind will result in arrest. I assure you that this is a temporary measure only, effective only until we are certain that our enemies are not using our technology to implement further violent attacks.

"In light of these requirements and the need to ensure public safety and to protect our children, effective immediately, I am declaring a state of martial law throughout the United States.

"Details of this declaration are being distributed to traditional media outlets and posted on official government websites. Please read them carefully and comply with their requirements.

"This has been, by far, the most terrible day in our nation's history. Cooperating together, we shall come through it and emerge stronger and more united. We shall be a single entity, one people, one nation, setting aside our quarrels of the past for the good of all.

"I thank you for your cooperation."

*Raqqa, Syria*

The screen went blank and the caliph sat back and laughed.

"Allah be praised, we have won!"

THE END

# William R. Forstchen

www.onesecondafter.com
www.dayofwrathbook.com
www.spectrumliteraryagency.com/forstchen.htm

William R. Forstchen is the author of over forty books, has a Ph.D. in history from Purdue University and is a Faculty Fellow at Montreat College. He has a broad spectrum of works including science fiction and fantasy, historical fiction, alternate history, several scholarly works, numerous short stories and articles and near-future novels ONE SECOND AFTER, PILLAR TO THE SKY and ONE YEAR AFTER. He is a *New York Times* bestselling author.

# Books by William R. Forstchen

ONE YEAR AFTER
DAY OF WRATH (novella)
PILLAR TO THE SKY
ONE SECOND AFTER
WE LOOK LIKE MEN OF WAR

*Lost Regiment series*
RALLY CRY
UNION FOREVER
TERRIBLE SWIFT SWORD
FATEFUL LIGHTNING
BATTLE HYMN
NEVER SOUND RETREAT
A BAND OF BROTHERS
MEN OF WAR
DOWN TO THE SEA

*Star Voyager Academy series*
STAR VOYAGER ACADEMY
ARTICLE 23
PROMETHEUS

ICE PROPHET
THE FLAME UPON THE IDE
A DARKNESS UPON THE ICE
INTO THE SEA OF STARS

*Wing Commander series*
ACTION STATIONS
FALSE COLORS
FLEET ACTION
HEART OF THE TIGER
THE PRICE OF FREEDOM
END RUN *with Christopher Stasheff*

*With Newt Gingrich*
THE BATTLE OF THE CRATER
VALLEY FORGE
TO TRY MEN'S SOULS
PEARL HARBOR
DAYS OF INFAMY
NEVER CALL RETREAT
GETTYSBURG
1945

*With Raymond Feist*
HONORED ENEMY

*With Greg Morrison*
CRYSTAL WARRIORS

*Star Trek: The Next Generation*
THE FORGOTTEN WAR

*Magic: The Gathering*
ARENA

*The Gamester Wars series*
THE ALEXANDRIAN RING
THE ASSASSIN GAMBIT
THE NAPOLEON WAGER

DOCTORS OF THE NIGHT
(Novella)